A
FATHER'S
LETTER

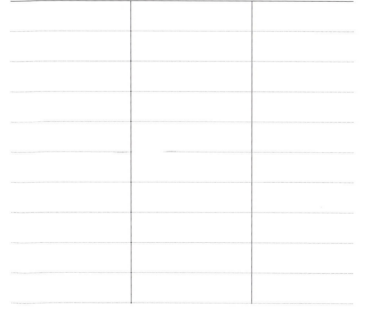

978-1-907179-00-0

A CIP catalogue for this book is available from the National Library.

Published by ORIGINAL WRITING LTD., Dublin, 2010.

Printed by CAHILL PRINTERS LIMITED, Dublin.

For my husband Philip, sons William and Colin,
Daughter-in-law Cofie.

I wish to acknowledge the encouragement and support of all my family while writing this novel

CHAPTER 1

1985

When the digger's jaw delivered the skull topsy-turvy onto the frozen bank of the lake, Joe Clancy groaned.

"Bad cess to it," he thought, "what a time to find a skull". He had booked a half-day off and had a million things to do because the following day he was away on holidays.

He looked across at Steve, the driver: "He'd make the most of it," Joe thought, "he'd be in the pub tonight regaling all and sundry about the find. Not the full shilling that fat bastard."

Human skeletons did not impress Joe one little bit, he had played and later worked at Glencarrig graveyard, where his father had been the gravedigger.

"That'll be Councillor Quint, Joe," his father's running commentaries were well remembered. "Lord have mercy! Thoughts might have entered his head but they didn't stay long; there was no room at all." His fingers would slip into the skull and would stir around. "No room at all," he would sigh, before throwing it dismissively on top of the mound of earth. When he spat on his hands it was time to start digging again.

"Bury it quick!" Joe yelled to Steve. He grabbed his shovel from the bank and ran towards the digger. "Bury that or we'll be stuck here all night," he hollered over the noise. "You've not forgotten? - I'm away tomorrow."

Steve turned the engine off; his ample body poured step by slow step down from the digger. A bubble of hot smelly air came with him. "Don't be silly Joe...I'm not doin' a thing like that. We've got to tell someone." Visible breaths merged above their heads.

"What for?" Joe whacked the window with his fist. "I knew you'd be like this," he spluttered with rage, "you're such a fecking..."

"Calm down!" Steve was more reproachful than angry. "It's a skull not a body; there'll be a bit of a stop, nothing much. I remember over at…" he broke off, Joe had walked away. "There's no need for all this fuss," he said more to himself than to Joe.

Joe moved out of earshot, up past rhododendrons and into the sunlight and full view of Tuskar Rock House. Known locally as "The Rock", it was built from stone quarried in Enniscorthy 200 years before. It was a solid-looking house with a two-Doric-pillared portico which cast a deep shadow over the lower part of the building. The hall-entrance door could not be seen from where Joe stood; it was a heavy substantial-looking oak door with metal hinges and bars. There was a vast expanse of lawn at the side of the house running away to a river bank of butchered bamboos below shivering poplar trees, from where occasional sounds of water came. The low sun shot rays up the lawn driving the early morning frost away. The house, at the higher end of the slope, loomed over the slowly changing patterns on the brightening grass as the air was warmed by passing day.

Joe knew that tragedy had struck this house years before. Time had clouded over the detail, but, as is often the case, the ordinary people had remained constant in their awareness of the extent, depth and intensity of the fearful events that had taken place. The events were given an existence which often became detached from what had actually taken place. The content was altered and retouched but the tragedy remained and marked the attitudes and feelings about the house, the place and the people who had been involved in the drama. The mullioned windows, hollow as the vacant sockets in the skull they had found, stared blankly back. Unbowed, forbidding, the house made Joe, not the most sensitive of creatures, feel that he was a trespasser. There was no doubt they were violating the place by cutting a road hardly two hundred yards from the house, robbing it of its dignified isolation. He moved back behind the bushes.

"Is that girl on the balcony?" Steve asked in a reconciliatory manner. Joe had been keen to talk about her earlier that morning.

"Don't be annoyin' me," Joe answered in a sulky voice. His mind still disturbed by the feeling of trespassing.

Mechanical rumblings continued in the background. In the distance their fellow road workers were laying tarmacadam; tar fumes filled their nostrils lessening Joe's appetite, though it was after midday. Earlier that morning Joe had been happy to get away from the fumes to go with Steve to demolish what looked like a simple outhouse. It had turned out to be more, extending as it did into the hillock. They had almost completed the job when Steve, digging under the building, had disturbed an unmarked grave, the hiding or resting place of an anonymous skull.

***

When the phone rang the Desk Sergeant took the call and then, as was his wont, shouted up the stairs to Superintendent Harry Furlong.

"They've found something near The Rock."

"What?" Superintendent Furlong hardly raised his voice.

"A skull!" the Sergeant called, "a skull at Tuskar Rock." he repeated.

The Superintendent straightened up and got to his feet. "Use the phone," he roared down the stairs, before shutting his door.

The phone rang.

"Superintendent Furlong." Harry Furlong was determined that his instructions be followed.

"It's me," the Sergeant seemed unruffled by the Superintendent's rigidity. "Seems it's been in the ground for ages. It was under an old building by the lake. The road gang's there at the moment, you know, and..."

"Well then, if they need someone at Tuskar, I'll go," Furlong said, " but that lot are such Neanderthals, it's most likely a sheep's head." But as he spoke he knew it would not be a sheep's head. He had a feeling of rising excitement and tension. It was not that Harry Furlong was an insensitive or particularly brash person but he had learned to make a clear distinction between his professional and non-professional life and to him the big house, its lands and appurtenances, its proprietors and occupants, its enemies and friends and neighbours now represented a conundrum, an unsolved problem, perhaps even an undetected crime. No feelings of awe or uneasiness would disturb him. Furlong was not a man who intruded; he was always, wherever he went, there of right. Trespassing was the shortcoming of others. The sound of feet stomping up the stairs and the flicker of someone advancing past the corridor windows of his office made Harry sigh. He hated people coming up uninvited. The sergeant thrust open the door and rested his body against the door frame.

"There's a fellah just come in... he's goin' mad downstairs. He wants to speak to you."

"What fellow?... for God's sake man I'm busy, get rid of him and use that phone!"

"If I'd used the phone he'd know you're here, you know...he'd be up those stairs himself, he's so mad." The Sergeant answered wearily with the air of a man who was very much put-upon.

For a moment the roar of a motor descending from the Market Square to the River Slaney carried to them and then the sounds of a car radio took over, thumping in their ears. The man downstairs shouted up "I want to see someone now, this instant."

Furlong glared at the Sergeant. "Who is it? Is he drunk?"

"No sir," the Sergeant straightened up, "it's Paddy Fitzwilliam, that's who... he's not drunk but, you know...I didn't recognise him at first..."

"Paddy Fitzwilliam!" The Superintendent looked astonished. "Wasn't he the boyfriend of the girl who drowned in Tuskar Lake..." The phone rang and Furlong picked it up, "must be nine or ten years ago?" he continued to address the Sergeant, while speaking into the phone; "Superintendent Furlong speaking," he then said, finally turning his attention to the mouthpiece.

"We're waiting ...over at Tuskar, Sir."

"Well then…I'll be there as soon as I can," Harry said to the voice on the phone.

"More like 30 years in the ground, if you ask me; the building under the hill was a shelter; built during the Suez… much older than the rest… nine or ten years can't be …," the voice continued.

Harry cut him short, "I'll be there." The receiver landed back on the phone. "Am I the last to be told of this find, Sergeant?"

"No Sir, I sent young Maguire out as I didn't want you going on a wild-goose chase, you know, and he rang back to say it was definitely a skull. That's when I informed you, Sir."

The self-righteous tone got on Harry's nerves. Too many "Sirs" in a sentence made him feel got at. He had given up years ago objecting to the "you know" that the Sergeant cluttered his sentences with, and a sardonic "NO, tell me!" only encouraged the Sergeant to do just that.

Superintendent Furlong signalled to the sergeant, "see to your man! Tell him I'll be down in a minute!"

As he waited Harry pulled at his eyebrows with soft long fingers. His high cheek bones and pale face coincided well with the austere man that he was. No one had ever heard him swear and even though he did occasionally raise his voice, it was always in order to cover a distance. This restraint seemed to instil greater fear into his crew than any robust shouting and swearing might have done. His mother, who had secretly worried he would become a priest, quietly rejoiced when he married in his teens. She waited in vain for a grandchild. Harry and Delia were a model couple in public, never alluding to any problem; very occasionally Delia would remark, in a faintly sneering way, that Harry had no friends. Harry, on the other hand, never spoke of his wife in a disparaging way: he would have considered such behaviour beneath him.

When the sergeant appeared again the Superintendent spoke as though thinking out loud. He was immediately back on the case that he had, not so much closed years before, as put to one side:

5

"All right then ... let's see now... that girl - Maurice Agan's elder daughter... She was taken from the lake near where they've just found the skull?" His eyebrows arched giving him a baboon-like appearance. "Yes Sir...everyone talked when the girl drowned. It was old Dr Keogh who examined the body. He told me so himself; I was on the desk that day, you know, that the girl hadn't eaten in days - dreadfully undernourished. Next day it was splashed all over the front pages of the local papers. The father abused poor old Doc for talking about his daughter." The sergeant talked at a gallop not drawing breath until he had exhausted all he had to say.

Harry was hunched over, deep in thought. He remembered it all too well. Eventually he looked up at the waiting Sergeant: "I'll be down immediately....Put Mr Fitzwilliam in the interview room."

As the Sergeant left, the door banged, shaking the plaster. Harry sighed again, pushed his chair away from his desk and rose to his feet. He was forced to ask himself, a hundred times a day - why these fellows were so rough? There was not a stick of undamaged furniture in the station, for they were the clumsiest force he had ever had to work with. He worried his finger around the door frame, checking for cracks. Automatically his hand went out to take his coat from the stand behind the door where it always hung; then, as was his wont, he stood surveying his refuge.

In the centre of the room stood his heavy black-oak desk and office chair, surrounded and protected by filing cabinets in a row two deep. Above the mantelpiece hung a painting of a currach out on the seas near Inishmore. In the picture men were fighting the dark water beneath a stormy sky. Grey horses reared on the land rising above the sea, and the men rowed on against the tide; their vigour raised Harry's heart. A second picture was hidden in a nook behind shelves. This painting, by Sir Luke Fildes of a gravely ill little girl, was a poignant reminder to Harry of the human condition. "In life we are in death," Harry often said to himself, especially when face to face with a dead body. A glance at this painting was not on his day to day check list of necessities, but he liked to renew his acquaintance with it frequently.

With his coat on his arm he glanced towards the little window that looked up to the tiny square of sky above Slaney Street. Gently he closed the door behind him.

***

When Harry entered the low-ceilinged room two storeys below, Paddy Fitzwilliam seemed to show surprise.

"You did want to see me, Mr Fitzwilliam, didn't you?" Furlong asked stiffly.

"Mr Fitzwilliam was just telling me he knows we've found something at The Rock."

"How does he know?"

"I got a phone call." Paddy Fitzwilliam snapped.

"Naturally he's upset; he thinks it might be his father, you know," the Sergeant explained.

"Naturally nothing! I'm not upset…and…I know it's him," Paddy said with emphasis. His manner was testy. He jerked a bony finger at the Superintendent. "I'm telling you it's my father, Tom Fitzwilliam." His accent was foreign, more mid-Atlantic than Irish, and his voice was thin, matching his gaunt face. "It's him… this is ridiculous; I've something to report to the police and they don't seem to want to know."

***

By the time Superintendent Furlong arrived at the lake the early March frost had melted in the bright afternoon sun. A gathering of road workers were sitting digesting their lunch among sprouting Primrose leaves and rubble. Commendably they had given themselves the afternoon off as a sign of respect.

After speaking to them the Superintendent set the garda technical unit to work. The road workers watched in fascination the careful sifting and separating of the earth and mud clods that they had thrown up. They chatted with the garda and together they speculated about the possible explanations for the present find. The technical unit could find nothing in the hardened mud except old bones and a leather, brass buckled, belt: no blood, hair or fibre to be collected. Owing to the amount of disruption left by the digger there was little for them to work on. They would take a photograph or two, then bag up the skeleton and be away within a couple of hours.

The Superintendent left his instructions and walked away around the dried up lake. The years that had passed had faded many memories; even the dead girl had not been in his mind for a while, but the house was different. Only recently he had dreamed he was pacing it's corridors, unable to escape. "Ridiculous!" he had thought, even as he dreamt. No doubt a therapist would say he was searching. Well now he had a find and an answer - of sorts. There had been a death at the lake, probably even before Anna's, that was what Maurice Agan's daughter had been called. Paddy Fitzwilliam was adamant the skeleton was his father; he was adamant about a lot of things! The Superintendent would have preferred a little doubt, a little wonder. It seemed too much like wanting to wrap things up before they had been properly examined. How the man had died, for instance and even why the man had died. Furlong could not say what the truth was, but he meant to find out.

Spinning on his heel he stared at the house: it had been built to dominate the surrounding area and when Maurice Agan was in residence there had been no opposition to contest this pretension. But times had changed: it would no longer be necessary to tread softly; he could now insist on answers. He had a skeleton; he was entitled to ask questions. Things were not as before: he had been laughed at, fobbed off and the worst offender in this had been his own boss, the Wexford man, Chief Superintendent Wright. Between Superintendent Wright and Mr Agan there had been a certain mutual esteem which had impeded the proper running of the enquiry and, in the same way, Furlong feared that he had been less diligent because Mr Agan was a man that he had respected. Had that poor child been let down?

Had she suffered? Terrible to think he might have done better. Well times had changed; affinities would now be ignored. This time he would stick to the principles of good policing. It was no part of his job to think in terms of friendship. Whether it be the word of a stranger or that of Mrs Agan would make no difference; both would be scrutinised. He had to find out what had been going on.

A girl appeared on the balcony above the portico. Behind her, curtains burst out from the open window flapping up to the gutters.

With the blustering of the wind came the darkening of the sky and Superintendent Furlong returned to the technical unit as the first drops of rain appeared. They made a quick retreat over the bank of primroses up to the gate known as the Kissing Gate. Following close behind the Superintendent heard his men discuss how they should proceed and the final decision was to lift the body bag over the gate. He saw the look of disquiet on a young guard's face, as the skeleton shifted in the bag above their heads. He wondered to himself whether at the same age he would have felt the same. He had a fairly down-to-earth attitude to death, but his approach had always been lenient towards those who showed fear, horror or disgust. He understood their predicament even if he did not share it.

On reaching his car, parked by the front entrance of the great house, he got a fleeting glimpse of the grown-up Liadan Agan disappearing from the balcony above his head. She was gone before he could acknowledge her presence. "Wasn't that just like her," he thought; he wanted a quick, unofficial word. Her flight brought to mind the phone call he had had all those years ago from her School Principal.

"She can be a bit imaginative with her tales and I wouldn't have thought much of it except she's started to be very positive about having seen a body," the Principal, Mrs Cleary, reported.

The Superintendent had then rung up Tuskar house and was told he could come almost immediately. When he arrived at the appointed time everyone seemed to be out, except for the girl,

Liadan Agan, and the cook Mrs Lucy Ryan. He remembered the child's face: round vacant eyes, expressive lips that twitched; her little hands that kept flying out in nervous gestures. An odd little body, immature for her years. Spoiled and encouraged to fantasise, he had suspected then - but now he knew better.

"Now Liadan... Liadan Agan... what a nice name!" (He tried to be gentle with her, but his deep voice dropped to a growl). "Why did you tell your teacher you'd seen someone dead by the lake?"

He waited while she swung about, making her shoes squeal, jumping on and off the lower steps of the stairs. When she had attempted to jump six in one go, flinging herself into the air, he had caught her and holding her tight, he had tried to force her to answer. "I don't know," she replied, a bemused look spreading over her face.

He placed her on the marble floor beside him and then she climbed the stairs again.

"*Anyway I didn't,*" she shouted defiantly.

Before he could react she was grabbed by the hand and marched up the stairs. "Leave her alone," Lucy Ryan, the cook, spoke so sharply her voice broke.

"Madam," he said, "I'm a police officer."

"Is that a fact?" Lucy looked witheringly at him.

They left him standing in the hall staring at a marble statue of Mercury. The figure held a torch above its head, lighting the stone stairs which curled gracefully past high windows to the floors above, where the servant and child had disappeared.

***

Harry leant against his car. It was all coming back to him: the to-ing and fro-ing, the frustration of getting nowhere. He stared at the house. One light shone from a downstairs window, but otherwise the house was dark. Clouds had gathered and thickened ominously; one or two drops of rain had fallen, but nothing more. The sun had disappeared behind the roof top and a bruise-like blue colour spread out from behind the black clouds.

Expecting the rain to come the birds did not seem much in the mood to sing; the early evening was still.

Again and again one thought returned to haunt the Superintendent: he should have done more all those years ago. Certainly he had sent in men with dogs to search along the lakeside but they had picked up nothing. As no one had been reported missing, how could he have gone on searching? The possibility that someone had died was all based on the uncertain report of a small child, who herself wandered from one version to another of what she had seen. But still, it had to be said, that even if the evidence had been stronger, his liking for the late Maurice Agan might have influenced the assiduousness with which he would have continued the investigation, and therefore, perhaps even as things had stood, he had missed something that he should not have missed. Later, after all the hoo-ha had died down, Maurice's older daughter Anna had drowned in the lake. God forbid there was a connection. Harry remembered how he had felt when he heard about the girl. In the end the Coroner brought in a verdict of death by misadventure. The Coroner had pointed to the fact that Anna's legs had been cut severely, "probably trying to disentangle herself from the reeds," he considered. Case closed: death by misadventure.

Then it had been said that Liadan had not seen a body by the lake at all, but had had a premonition of her sister's death. Everything nicely tied up: everyone happy.

But not Harry! He did not believe in premonitions. He had returned several times to the house after Anna's death, but he never came away any the wiser. Liadan had talked in riddles and her father, Maurice, was always inebriated. Liadan always looked well looked-after; he had presumed that Felicity, the girl's stepmother, saw to that, or perhaps and more likely, the impervious cook, Lucy.

The family had left for Italy a couple of months after the funeral. No one had blamed them.

**

Harry Furlong got into his car and drove away from the house down the sweep to the iron gates all the time continuing his ruminations. He had never believed in the idea of the perfect crime, and had always argued that it was only an excuse for a badly-run investigation.

In the Autumn of 1974 the sniffer dogs has searched the lake side for signs of dead bodies. Anna died in 1975, early on in the year. He remembered clearly because he and Delia, his wife, had moved house. She had given him a lot of stick, accusing him of revelling in the misery of others, instead of helping her with the move. It was true that he had been preoccupied and worried that something had remained undetected. He knew she had good reason to be irritated, but there was no excuse for that sort of talk.

Liadan must now be eighteen, he decided; he thought her not more than eight when he had sent the dogs in. The young girl had witnessed a death at the lake and she had tried to tell people. No one believed her. Perhaps this was why she had not come down to see him. But would she corroborate Paddy Fitzwilliam's account about that day in 1974. Would anyone? When he had the forensic reports he would come back. Superintendent Harry Furlong drove the couple of miles back to the station in Templeslaney.

CHAPTER 2

1974

The summer morning was filled with bright, white light. The air was fresh. By midday the sun would be hot and the sky veiled with haze. As the heat of the day increased, the dew dried quickly and a low mist appeared over the grass giving it a bleached appearance. The first sounds of the grasshopper filled the air, and Tuskar Rock House turned to a lighter shade of grey in the sunlight.

Liadan ran by her father's side. They came through the orchard and approached the lake from the south side. Liadan knew what her father's purpose was; she knew his ways so well. She knew that once out of the orchard they would creep through the beech trees, up and over the bank and before the workmen became aware or could react, Maurice would have caught them idling - sleeping or chatting. Liadan was undecided whether to annoy her father by causing a rumpus or watch the workmen's discomfort when they were caught. He was grumpy enough already, she decided.

"Why are you letting the water out?" she asked instead.

He squeezed her hand and let it go. For each step Maurice took Liadan took three. She grabbed his hand, pulling him back, trying to delay him.

"I have to remake the dam, it's leaking," he said not looking at her. "I've told you we're digging the blasted lake out... it's leaking. I'm sick of telling people. We're doing it a bit early because it's leaking.... nothing sinister about that," his voice rose.

"But we can't swim Daddy," Liadan scowled at him determined to show he wasn't the only one in a bad mood. Her big sister Anna had gone off with Wendy. Wendy Leigh, having many sisters of her own seemed to have a rather jaundiced view of little sisters, or so Liadan felt. Wendy never wanted her

13

around. Today no one had come to play. She was bored. Felicity, Maurice's friend, would lecture if Liadan complained to her, "*educated* people never get bored," Liadan mimicked, mouthing the words to herself, her lips turned down like a clown's. Lucy would want her to bake scones. This was the sort of thing she had to put up with and nobody seemed to realize.

"I'm bored, I want to do something," she grumbled.

"Shush Lia," Maurice answered automatically; he was not listening anymore, Liadan could tell. He seemed to be totally indifferent to her feelings and she did not like it. His bad temper was increasing as he got closer to the work site; it now reached such a pitch that he started to rant; he was rehearsing the verbal chastising that someone was going to receive. The thought of the expected wrong-doing spiralled him out of control.

Scornfully Liadan watched her father's anger growing. He was swearing now under his breath as he ascended the hill before her, and by the time that she joined him at the top his accusations had found a definite target: Paddy Fitzwilliam was sitting on his barrow near the dam. Standing close to her father she waved to Paddy excitedly. Maurice stood still, his ranting had ceased but he was burning with suppressed and reined-in fury.

"Get on you lazy loafer," he raged under his breath. "Bloody Fitzwilliam…oh they had to saddle me with him."

Liadan tugged at his hand, but she did not need to worry. Paddy could not hear above the noise of the machine. The big bully in Maurice would calm down before he was within earshot. He was well aware of the boundaries over which he could not step when dealing with the neighbour's son; these neighbours were friends of Felicity and therefore, by extension, were presumed to be friends of his.

Liadan knew he wanted to keep "in" with Felicity.

***

"A truly exceptional person," he had told Lucy and Liadan in the kitchen that morning when he knew for certain that Felicity was within earshot. Even the child, Liadan, understood her father's manoeuvring to please the woman who lived in his house.

Lucy unable to endure his pathetic earnestness snorted and sneered: "Is that a fact?" The whites of her eyeballs appeared fleetingly beneath her half-closed eyelids matching her derisive tone. She swept the plates and mugs from the table with her large red hands, placing them noisily in the dishwasher, "Well, we're much too busy," she added irrelevantly

"Why? " Liadan had asked him, "What does that mean?"

"Well you might ask," Lucy had said.

"It means...she..." he had muttered weakly, "oh you know very well ..."

Maurice was a heavy man with thick, red, unruly hair. "Like an orang-utan, Lia," he liked to say, "but not so good-looking." He had sensitive milky blue eyes and a Roman nose. His lower jaw was strong but weakened by the presence of a cleft chin. His disposition was volcanic but kept in check by his need to be liked. It might have surprised some people that Maurice did actually exercise any control, but then there was a lot more there to control than these same people would have believed: Maurice's temper was vile and he was certainly capable of inflicting physical damage when he lost it.

Liadan had never in her life been frightened of him; in her eyes he was often a very silly Daddy but one whom she could manage very well.

***

She set about her task now expecting the usual victory.

Maurice seemed temporarily lost in thought, trying to find some way to vent his ill-humour without any collateral damage. The child became tired of waiting; her father should not ignore her for so long:

"Daddy, Daddy!" Liadan jerked at his hand with both of hers and, because he did not heed her, she kicked out at him, "Can we swim tomorrow?"

A large hand deflected her kicking foot and he palmed her away, righting her with the other as she stumbled. "Anna will take you…to the sea…. you can't swim here." He did not seem to concentrate on what he said to her and all the time his voice grew louder.

"You're breaking the bank, you fools," he roared at the workmen. "You'll turn the tractor over, you bloody fools." He let Liadan's hand drop and started running down to the pebbled shore which was slowly increasing in size as the lake-water trickled away through the broken bank.

Liadan dropped onto the grass: not much point in shouting at him, he would not heed her. No one could control him now. He had reached the workmen.

From her vantage point she could see fingers of stony, dried earth pointing to the centre of this lower section of the lake; the upper lake-water glinted through a wall of birch. Over her right shoulder red crocosmia plants were in bloom, their flowery stems bowed towards the lake. Although there was no possibility from where the child was of seeing either the entrance to an air-raid shelter beside the lake or the shores beyond, the exaggerated loop that the path took suggested some kind of large obstruction. Trees and shrubs hid the house from view. It was like being in a secret world. She was out of sight of Felicity and Lucy and their endless instructions.

Liadan was a child who lived to a great extent in a world of her own. Like all children, if somewhat more so, she slipped in and out of the current of activity around her: when she was in, she happily and robustly took part, but her life apart from it and her constant observation of it made her a strange little being who knew and understood far more than she was ever given credit for.

As she sat she heard her father hollering at the workmen over the noise of the tractor. The tractor moved forward and the men dug out the reeds shovelling them into a trailer from whence they were deposited into the ditch beyond the dam. Paddy followed with barrows of round stones which he toppled on to the cleaned out lake bed. They made slow progress, overcome by the heat of the day.

Long white grasses prickled the soft skin at the back of Liadan's knees, and she moved on to her tummy. She plucked a dandelion clock and blew the seeds without counting; her thoughts were busy. After much musing she concluded that Maurice was no longer the indulgent father she had been used to, of late his mind always seemed occupied elsewhere. Not once recently had he tried to comfort her when she was upset, to cheer her up and make her laugh again. And the lake - everything about the lake made her and Anna happy, but again recently, not Maurice; something was upsetting him.

Too soon Maurice was beside her again.

"Come Lia," he said, not looking at her, his eyes watching the lake. "That bloody family....," he complained, his mind on Paddy, or more significantly, Paddy's family.

"You're always giving out," Liadan protested. She knew what family he was referring to. Everyone liked Paddy, even her father must; she was sure.

She waved to Paddy.

"Aren't you coming?" Paddy waved his arms, beckoning her.

Liadan sniffed the air; the strong smell of rotting vegetation wafted to her and she found it strangely agreeable, but she gripped her nose between her thumb and finger in an exaggerated way. She did not want Paddy to know she liked the unpleasant smell, and there was no possibility of pretending she could not smell it. Paddy made her feel that she wanted to be grown up; on most days he was her favourite person in the world. He was friendly and happy to play with her, even though she was not big like Anna and Wendy. He had floppy black hair and a funny smile. Occasionally Maurice would slap him on the shoulder and tell him he was a fine fellow, but that was before... She vaguely wondered why things seemed to have changed between Maurice and Paddy. She was used to her father's lightning changes of humour and opinion, but usually, although she was still so young and because she had always felt so close to her father, she understood to some extent the reasons behind his apparently unpredictable and erratic judgements. This time however she was at sea.

17

"Come on, you'll get used to it," he shouted, "Look at the baby eels!"

And before Maurice could stop her she dashed away to Paddy, then on to below the dam where the water drained from the lake. Like an excited puppy she ran backwards and forwards trying to find an easy way down to the escaping water in the bottom of the ditch.

"Oh Paddy I haven't got anything to catch them in," she screamed. A ball of wriggling eels slid from the drainage pipe dropping a couple of feet into the muddy ditch.

"Oh Paddy, they're escaping."

She lowered herself onto her tummy; she lay on the steep slope her feet pointing upwards, balancing precariously, dragging herself to the water's edge. Paddy appeared above her.

"You'll get into trouble Lia; you're getting filthy...if you're lucky Felicity'll still be at our house."

"Oh is she having lunch there?" Liadan asked with a hopeful look in her eye. "Anyway I don't care." she said firmly, but nothing about her looked sure. She tried to move to a less muddy area but, being almost upside down, trying to right herself made her slip a bit further towards the edge.

"You look like an eel," Paddy laughed.

"You look like a ..."

"Very funny," Paddy cut in before Liadan could think of something rude to say.

"I wish you'd start filling the lake again," she said.

"Then I'd have to leave. Maurice said there'd be no more work for me once the lake's cleared. In three months time I'll be gone to Kenya anyway, chasing rhinos not little girls and I know which'll be easier," he said in a teasing, sleepy way.

"Oh Paddy," she said feeling sad. "I wish you didn't have to go."

"I'll miss coming here, really I will." his voice dipped. He sat on the bank above her. "It's so hot today, the very thought of going to a hotter climate is unbearable."

Liadan nodded her head sagely; she knew he would miss them very much.

Under a beech tree he lay down. The dappled light broke up on him in blurred moving shapes. A trickle of sweat inched its way down his face gradually, drying before another ran after it. The warm air lay heavy on them and while his eyes shut out the scene around him the constant chatter from the little girl drifted on.

"Anna says you're going to look after sick animals."

A smile broke on his drowsy face.

"Why can't you look after them here?" As no answer came from above Liadan continued.

"Daddy says the man who looks after our horses is demented, and I don't think that's good."

The silence from the bank continued and Liadan looked up through the grass, noticing how spiky the blades were, and how much nearer the daisy heads seemed to be to the sky. She peered through them at Paddy bringing him into focus. He looked asleep. With a deep sigh she switched her attention back to the eels. On inspection their bodies seemed slimy but she poked them with her thumbs before chancing a squeeze with her fingers.

The sun caught her arms and legs turning them pink. Minutes raced by like the water she was playing in and then suddenly she found herself lifted onto her father's shoulders.

"No!" she squealed at him.

"I told you an hour ago that we had to go back to the house," he said crossly.

She gripped his neck with her dirty hands and dug her heels into his chest. "Where's Paddy?"

"Gone...good God Lia! You're choking me."

"Gone where?" She asked releasing her grip a little.

"How should I know...lunch I expect. Felicity wants us back now. We must hurry."

"She's at Paddy's house, so she won't mind," and because he put her on the ground a bit roughly she continued as if he had questioned her. "That's what Paddy said."

No further words were necessary, Maurice was in another rage. Liadan accepted it without fully understanding, and she was not perturbed. She sang to herself. The hungry feeling that was growing in her stomach urged her to keep up with Maurice as he strode ahead. "Oh well," she thought, "I'll have to go and wash my hands and probably change my clothes if Felicity is at home, because she will suggest it and Daddy will insist that I do whatever she wants." While this thought was occupying her mind she found herself being lifted and dumped on the steps up to the hall door. Then Maurice was in his car driving away from the house, the engine of the car screeching, pebbles shooting out from the back wheels and the tyres making a tearing noise on the gravel.

"Driving like "that word" off a shovel. That's what Lucy would say," thought Liadan. "She thinks I don't know what she'd like to say. Shit, shit, shit," she sang under her breath.

Liadan pushed the hall door and as she hoped all the right smells greeted her.

"Liadan, change and wash," Felicity commanded as she came in. "*Look at the state of you.* I'll *really* have to have a word with your father."

"He's gone to town in his wellies." Liadan answered quickly trying to divert the attention from herself.

Liadan could not remember her mother, but she was sure that she had not been like Felicity. Even though she often thought it would be nice to have a mother to talk to, she found that Lucy could more or less fill this gap. She did not really suffer from her mother's absence. She imagined what her mother must have been like and she had invented a sort of guardian angel to whom she could resort when the everyday going got too difficult and her problems required more imaginative solutions than those supplied by the kitchen and the drawing room. Liadan often talked to her imaginary mother before she fell asleep and her mother's answers would soothe her into happy dreams. Liadan and her mother saw eye to eye on every matter and no mother and daughter lived in greater harmony.

Felicity stood by the hall table opening letters. Liadan usually did not notice how Felicity was dressed but today she noticed that she was wearing a sleek black and white summer dress with elegant high heel shoes, the sort Liadan wished she could wear.

Liadan eyed them enviously. When Felicity struck the gong, Liadan instantly forgot about the shoes. Felicity's generally impassive face showed intense wrath at the moment the gong stick hit its target. She looked wicked, like a witch. Liadan shuddered; her nose seemed sharp and her chin stuck out more - but no point in dawdling. Lucy would open the hatch between the kitchen and the dining-room and if Liadan had not changed, both of them would tick her off. How strange, Felicity had not asked why Maurice had gone to town. "She always seems to know everything," Liadan thought.

Felicity walked sedately to the serving hatch in the dining-room wall. "Lucy, put Mr Agan's lunch in the oven. Keep it hot for 10 minutes, no longer," she instructed.

An "Mmm" came from the kitchen in response.

"Make sure you do, Lucy, *no spoiling* him."

"Spoiling is it... he's a right in his own house, I suppose," Lucy spoke to the oven but just loud enough to be heard.

By the time Liadan had changed and collected the plates from the hatch Felicity was seated in Maurice's place with her back to the bay window which formed almost one complete wall of the room. She would supervise and instruct Liadan on points of table etiquette; Liadan just knew. If Maurice had been there Liadan would have been allowed to eat in the kitchen with Lucy. Things were all out of joint that day.

The bay window had been opened early that morning allowing the warm air to flow into the room. Thick walls insulated the house so that often, on a hot summer's day, the house remained cool and only warmed a little if the windows were opened. Though out of view, the sounds of falling water from Felicity's new fountain could be heard, a constant reminder of how many things Felicity had changed since she had come to stay.

"You'll see," she said when she first came, "chance has no place here, *design, innovation, order*," Maurice had smirked with pleasure. Liadan had told Lucy he looked silly. Lucy said, "That one's no amadán, she's her foot in...she'll stay for good."

"Sit up straight Liadan." Felicity's voice was crisp. "*What* have you been doing this morning?"

Liadan groaned. Umpteen times every day she wished that Anna would not spend so much time with the miserable Wendy Leigh. Then, with a bit of luck, she might have been sitting there doing the talking.

"There is lots of eels in the lake and I'm going to collect them," Liadan answered grudgingly.

"There are," Felicity corrected. "I really can't understand why you girls like swimming in that *awful* lake. I do *worry* you'll catch something."

"I would love to catch a lot of eels and put them in your fountain." Liadan thought to herself, but she remained silent.

CHAPTER 3

1984

The early morning sun streamed through the iron-barred kitchen window, filling the room with light. Liadan sat at the kitchen table eating her breakfast, her feet resting on the wooden rung of the table. Spoonful by slow spoonful the porridge travelled towards her mouth, as though laden with a heavy sense of what lay ahead. Today she would get the letter from her father. It was her birthday; she was eighteen.

All the last few months she had been so torn and troubled by what she knew this day must bring. She had known her father better than anyone and she feared that even with the reading of the letter there would be no certainty about all the dreadful events that had filled her growing years.

Out of the corner of her eye she could see Lucy watching her and she purposely looked away through the open window, refusing Lucy's smiles. House martins caught her eye as they flew to feed their young in the bell tower at the other side of the enclosed yard and then Charley, the yard man, appeared. He set about feeding the animals. Gad, the donkey Anna had loved, he fed last.

"That dumb brute," was Charley's constant complaint to Lucy, "stood on my foot again."

But Lucy would have none of it, "You're always under some-one's feet."

The sunshine joined forces with the heat of the kitchen and Lucy spoke brusquely: "Buck up love, it's your birthday. If you don't like anything you can change it...herself wouldn't care." - 'herself' meaning the now Mrs Felicity Agan.

"I loved everything...I told you...it's not that," Liadan's voice sounded flat. "The solicitor's coming today, that's all."

"Don't see the silly man! You don't have to. Not on your birthday."

"But Luce...I must. He's coming especially, with more of Daddy's papers. I want to get it over with."

"Is that a fact?"

"For God's sake," Liadan snapped.

Lucy's left arm cleaned the Aga's cream-coloured tops, while her right hand clasped her hip. It was a bad sign and promised someone a tongue lashing.

Up above her head hung hooks, levers and pulleys, some wired to copper bells. "I'll have to have a go at them in the next few days," she said with emphasis, changing the topic, as she thought, seamlessly. The copper bells above the Aga shone down on her. "Not today! It's going to be stifling." Winter and summer Lucy kept the range burning, no matter how they all suffered in the heat.

Lucy was as tall as a tree, according to the young Liadan, slim, bendy, with hands as strong as Charley's. She had eyes like marbles, bright-blue, hard, dirt-detecting eyes. First thing that morning she'd scrubbed the slate floors; the bane of her life it was, she said; but she would never hear of her slate floor being replaced. Now it gleamed a multi-shaded black. Lucy clung to her kitchen and all its arrangements with unrelenting tenacity. It was as though she herself had grown up there and in a sort of way she had: she had come originally as a very young girl to work and she had developed her method of running the active little world around her in the rooms that made up the kitchen, scullery and larders. She did not intend ever to give up her domination of this space and it had been a fight when Felicity moved in. After twenty years she considered the kitchen to be her own and would brook no interference. Everything had to stay: the old-fashioned hatches, the ancient doors scraping the stone floors along the scullery passage. Fine, solid doors, they opened into places like the butler's pantry, which might have been lifted straight from the 19th Century, with its old dressers and wooden churn. Even the vast flour bin by the pantry door (big enough for the girls to hide in when they were small) had to stay exactly where it was. In Lucy's view one could tell its quality from the sound it made when the cover was slammed down and she liked to knock on the wood and remark within Felicity's hearing "None of your flimsy modern rubbish here, thank God."

But it was the array of outlandish equipment hanging from the ceiling in the main kitchen which caused the most conflict. Felicity protested, "So *unhygienic* Lucy...*Quite* medieval," but to no avail. Lucy was resolute, the day Felicity touched her kitchen was the day she would go home and "not be up that avenue again."

"What do you want for your lunch? I'll do something special. Your birthday cake's in the tin ...all ready. Herself was nowhere to be seen this morning when a little help wouldn't 'a done any harm... pottering in the garden no doubt. That one can't leave well enough alone." Lucy never bothered to hide her animosity.

"I'm sure I'll manage." Lucy would have said if Felicity Agan had come to help. Felicity's role was simply to be the recipient of Lucy's bad humour.

Liadan knew to defend Felicity would be pointless.

"Anyone who doesn't like kittens... well you can't trust them, can you love? The other day the new kitties were having a sip of milk by the kitchen door... that one made such a hullabaloo! Said she'd kick them out herself if I didn't, and she would have too," Lucy said.

Liadan shook her head. "She hates cats."

"And they hate her," Lucy said as if both were of equal stature.

"Will you be able to find homes for them?" Liadan asked, sounding more concerned than she felt. She was usually fairly indifferent to the cats, mostly because there were so many of them and they had always been there. She never examined them in detail or called them by name.

"Oh yes, most nice people like cats."

Maurice had not been the slightest bit bothered about the cats in the yard, Liadan remembered, but somehow Lucy managed not to dwell on that.

Lucy attacked the tops again, this time she used both hands to clean. Liadan smiled. The deep affection she felt for Lucy always remained unspoken and seemed unrecognised; no one, least of all Lucy, considered it necessary to draw attention to such things. Lucy had dedicated her life to the well-being of the Agan family and they were grateful; that seemed to be the extent of it. If Liadan had decided to leave and live in a distant part of the world, she would not have consulted Lucy about the matter. Perhaps if Lucy had become ill, she would return, but then again perhaps not. Liadan remembered that a couple of months after Maurice's death she had teased Lucy because she had cried more than anyone, and Felicity had called her, "a *veritable* bog."

"Did you love him, Luce?"

"Of course...admired him too."

"Yes, but did you...," and she hugged her shoulders while she kissed the air.

"Get out of my kitchen with your stupid talk," Lucy snapped.

The callous fifteen-year-old Liadan had pealed with laughter, but the eighteen-year-old now thought Lucy's love was special.

"I'll be fine. I don't need too much fussing. When I have seen what there is to fix up in Daddy's affairs I will begin to enjoy the day" she said in her sweetest voice, putting her arms around Lucy's shoulder, but Lucy was determined to fuss.

"Are you sure, Love?" she fretted.

I'm going upstairs," Liadan said at last, "I'll be fine...For God's sake give it a rest, "she broke into a laugh, fending off Lucy's fresh attempts to mother her.

***

At Anna's bedroom door Liadan hesitated and then crossed the corridor between Anna's room and her own. But neither refuge suited her mood and she continued along the corridor, down five steep steps to old Nanny Betty's rooms. Three rooms were Nanny's realm: the school-room, her bathroom and her bedroom. She had slept isolated from the rest of the household, to the relief of all concerned. She was strict and she was snobby and rigid, but she was good with the girls and a tartar with adults. If the girls needed to hide from Maurice they went to Nanny's room, knowing no matter what mischief they had got up to Maurice would never follow them there. Betty had gone years before and Liadan did not associate any pain with losing her. She traced her fingers over the painted butterflies on their old schoolroom wall. She didn't like to think too much of Anna, but when it did happen she allowed herself to think in the present tense. "The blue butterflies are Anna's favourites", she would say, imagining herself talking to Nanny. Anna had seen the rare blue Irish butterflies at the lake when she was swimming. She seemed to have a fire in her that flared up at the wonders that she perceived around her. All these wonders were then immediately recorded in her painting. She never allowed anything that gave her joy or pause to go undepicted and so the old schoolroom and her bedroom were a chronicle of the girl's impressions, enthusiasms and joys.

"I know!" Liadan spoke aloud to the room, "It's silly to talk to oneself."

***

By the time the afternoon arrived Liadan had reconciled herself to the solicitor's visit; but then instead of the older Mr Dalkey, his son arrived. She had known Ronan Dalkey for years. They had never got on – there had always been too much youthful rivalry. She could hardly bear to have him there. He lacked the gravitas of the occasion. She wanted someone paternal in control: he would not do. He did not have to face the past; he should not have access to a letter from a father who had died, and she did not want him breathing down her neck, gaping at her.

How could he know that it scared her to think of what her father might have written? The dead body worried her but she had been sure for many years that there was a dead body somewhere in the lake. Her fear was of the turmoil she would feel as she read her father's emotional outpourings. Had it been someone of her father's age, she knew that there would be a greater sympathy and understanding of the situation: Ronan was too green, too young.

At first they sat silently by the window in the drawing-room. There was nothing but water on the table and she did not offer him anything else. She wanted to tell him to go; she wanted to leave herself. It felt like an age but it was only a few seconds.

"You know it all anyway," her father had promised her. But Liadan knew that this was not the case. She turned towards the window to gaze down the lawn into the distance to where the bamboo ran wild beneath the poplar trees. The fleeting shadows were there of her and Anna playing. The bamboo rafts that they had once made and floated on the river now lay, with arrows and fishing rods, like scattered debris from a flood. Woven willow branches used as paddles sprouted new green shoots and grew into living sculptures. One dumped by the lakeside now appeared high in a birch tree where a heron made her nest. Beyond the poplars the River Galley flowed. Liadan could remember lying on her front, still and expectant, careful not to throw her shadow onto the river, watching shoals of minnows soak up the warmth of the sun. Further down there were stepping-stones, light grey-dead or washed shining black as the water splashed, leaving tiny diamonds of light. Maurice had rolled the stones into place in order to cross the widened river. He had shown the girls how to build crannogs; he staked the riverbed, adding reeds and mud to make their own island. Thick strong brier stems bolted along old trails deep into the wood.

Felicity came to the window placing a basket of fresh mint on the stone sill. She waved to both of them, and they both waved back in unison, but Liadan realised there was nothing united in their two faces: Ronan looked wary and Liadan could not gauge just how crazy she must look, but she could guess; she knew she wasn't behaving normally. She tried to bring back the old cheeky Liadan that Ronan would have known, but she couldn't quite manage to ask, "Wha...have I got something belonging t' you?" to curb his stares.

"There are a couple of documents for you to sign," Ronan's voice broke in on her confusion. He put the folder down: "Also a letter."

It was a shock to see her name in her father's handwriting. Again she turned away. Seeing his writing brought him back to her completely. His large hand holding the pen or pencil, his heavy breathing as he concentrated on manoeuvres that should have been so difficult for such large hands and yet were executed with the utmost precision. She remembered so often climbing on to his knee with a sharpened pencil, a sheet of white paper and a request:

"Daddy, please draw us something."

Anna would lean against his shoulder or the back of the arm-chair; Liadan would seat herself on the wide arm of the chair; Maurice would straighten himself up and taking a book from the nearby shelf, rest the blank page on it and begin to draw.

The children knew that they were to guess what it was that he was drawing – it was all part of the fun. It was almost always an animal – but what animal, and what was the animal doing?

He would start with the point of a back foot raised in the air and draw an outstretched leg swelling out to form the hind-quarters; then he would lift his pencil and bring it back to the paper, beginning on a foot that still remained on the ground, and with gentle and firm lines bring it upwards swelling out into a body; then long lines to make an outstretched body and a strong, thick neck ending in the slim, fine nose of a …. a moment of doubt and then he would add the hooked front limbs which completed the movement.

"A fox being chased," Anna would screech, and Liadan would nestle down to watch him complete the delicate little ears and large, bushy tail: a simply perfect fox flying away from the hounds behind him.

**

Ronan and his father had arrived the day after Maurice's death. Sean Dalkey, Ronan's father, had spoken on the phone to Felicity, "Ronan'll take Liadan horse-riding or whatever...take her mind off things," he had said, without bothering to wonder if Liadan wanted this. "Besides I have to see you, there are details in his will you'll have to know about."

The memories flooded in.

His body lying on the mahogany bed, his red hair arranged on the embroidered pillow. A crucifix hung above the bed and a collection of silver candlesticks with lighting candles stood over the corpse casting a yellow light. Lace covers fell to the floor shrouding the bed. She stretched out to touch his face but it was changed by gravity into an austere mask, and she snatched her hand back.

Lucy cut a lock of his hair for Liadan's locket.

"A memento, Love."

Liadan shuddered, she shook her head. She really did not want his hair.

* * *

Ronan's eyes followed her as she walked to and fro. Her mind was all over the place. No wonder he stared. Her father's handwriting on the envelope that lay on the table tormented her. Ronan picked the envelope up again as if intending to force her to take it.

* * *

She should not have been there! She had walked in unexpectedly to see Felicity slicing deep into her father's wrist with a carpet cutter. No testimony of life gushed out, only a slight ooze of pale yellow translucent liquid fell on to the towel beneath; his heavy arm slipped from Felicity's grasp and flopped over the edge of the bed. A howl hovered in Liadan's head, her mouth opened wide in a silent scream, and a sweet taste filled it. She stood transfixed, only her eyes moved.

"No!..." she managed.

Felicity looked up." Darling *what are you* doing?"

"What are YOU doing?" she screamed before being convulsed in sobs.

"I meant why did you come in?" Felicity kept her voice calm.

"Maurice made me promise."

"Liar!" Liadan screamed, "liar!"

***

Liadan had had no glimpse of Anna when her father carried her body from the lake. Liadan had been too young to face the enormity of her death; Anna had been too young to die. Five years later her father had died and now three years after that he was going to tell her everything. She pushed her hair back from a faint scar on her forehead. With a weak smile she took her chair opposite Ronan.

He had changed from the skinny, all-Adam's-apple kind of gawky boy she remembered going riding with that day. But still she would have recognised him. Unchanged were his clear blue-green eyes and tight blackberry coloured hair. He had the sort of face people found handsome: well-structured, even and clear. As he moved back in his seat he crossed his long legs knocking the table and almost upsetting the jug of water. One large hand held the table as it rocked while the other grabbed the jug, and the smile that he turned to Liadan reminded her so much of the days when they had played together. As Ronan looked about the room Liadan's eyes followed his.

"So much is different since I was here," he said, "even the pictures aren't the same." It might have seemed a dangerous topic but he spoke with such ease that Liadan smiled.

Above the piano, hung a painting of her father; he looked steadily ahead, out onto the garden: a big soft man with mild eyes and a smile of contentment on his lips.

"I remember the first time I met your father he scared me to death. He was roaring like King Kong, a lot of blasting and damning and then you came out of the bushes and told him to shush. Well I thought you'd be in trouble, but he turned in an instant into the man in the painting."

Liadan had often wondered whether other children found her father as fascinating as she and Anna did. Sometimes she felt that some were afraid of him but were drawn to him by his wonderful understanding of what children really liked: he built tree houses, he drew pictures and he told wonderful stories and it was very rare that his ill-humour, which was so easily provoked, was turned against them.

"Poor Daddy!" Liadan laughed. "I think he frightened every child who came to play, until they learnt his rages were never aimed at them."

A smaller painting of Anna stood on the piano. Not the traditional portrait, more a flight of fancy. Surrounded by butterflies, she appeared to walk on air. Her arms were raised to welcome the tiny creatures and her face shone with joy. There was a shadow of something indefinable caught in the painting. But this was not visible to everyone.

A dog barked, distracting Ronan, and he turned away from the pictures, following the sound from the riverbank below the level of the lawn.

"The garden too is so changed," he said. "I hardly recognize any of it. Aunt Julia said I wouldn't. She's mad about gardening."

"Oh, it's Felicity..."

"I've had strict instructions to keep my eyes open! But I'm not good with plants."

"Your aunt ought to come and see for herself. Felicity loves showing it off."

There was a short silence, which seemed more like an age to Liadan. She was loath to lean over and take the letter and Ronan did not refer to it again. It lay between them.

Liadan slipped off her shoes, tucked one bare foot under her bottom and tried to make herself feel ready. She held her pink toes in her hand like a child. As her head hung down her hair gleamed, catching rods of gold light against slim pink-brown shoulders. It swished back and forth. Recollections of playing

by the lake with Anna came flooding into the room; recollections of Wendy, of Ronan and, of course, her dear Paddy; she
could almost hear their voices. She wondered then if Ronan
thought of how she, the baby sister, had outgrown the older -
especially today. Anna would never grow old; she would always
remain seventeen.

Felicity's voice floated in from the veranda through the open
French window.

"Let's have tea out here Lucy," she called, and a moment
later they heard Wendy say:

"I don't think she's heard; I'll go and tell her"

And then, clear as a bell, Felicity's scoffing voice, "*of course*
she did; she was at the bedroom window."

CHAPTER 4

1984

Generally people found Mrs Felicity Agan an alarming woman, but there were a number of men who found her enigmatic. Often they were the same sort of men who, in their vanity, thought that she would find them irresistible and that an ordinary fellow would not have a chance with her. To her friends her aloofness became a part of what they admired. Liadan seemed to be much in awe of her, as her father had been, and they were the people who knew her best.

Felicity cultivated this feeling of uncertainty in those that surrounded her by occasionally appearing to be very accessible and then, without warning, removing herself to a haughty distance, from which she seemed to rain down judgement on those around her.

"If Felicity Agan hadn't been such a handful… a little too deep for the likes of me," Sean Dalkey said with such modesty that Ronan had to suppress a derisive snort, "I'd have been tempted. I met her years ago in Dublin... charming woman." His head wiggled about in an embarrassing dance. "Of course Maurice didn't like me talking about those days." Sean became lost in happy memories. After a moment or two he seemed to recollect something unpleasant, and shaking his head he warned, "Take my word for it, what is true of the goose is true of the gosling; Liadan is a chip off the old block."

"They're not related," Ronan pointed out.

"No, but they're teacher and pupil," Sean said.

"You're forgetting I know her better than you."

"She's grown up now... you'll see."

***

But he had not seen: a frivolous attribute like charm could not do justice to Liadan and there was nothing haughty about her.

The fact was, though Ronan would have denied it vehemently, he could never see the faults that were there; his view of her was idealistic. He thought her deep; he thought her clever. He believed that she would remain interesting for ever. He looked with delight at her determined chin and courageous eyes and felt currents of contentment and happiness run through him. He loved her pink toes and her sun-filled hair. He had almost forgotten the reason why he was there. He tried to restrain his feelings and to concentrate on hers, but he was excited and even elated. This was his first meeting with her since Maurice's funeral - and if he had allowed himself - he might have fallen in love. But it was impossible, inappropriate. He had no intention of staying in Templeslaney and no desire for commitment.

A slightly awkward pause in the proceedings made him reach for his briefcase; he opened it knowing he would be peering into an empty space. Should he pick the letter up and offer it to her again? Perhaps he should look busy, give her time and she would take the letter herself. He wished he had something to say. Yesterday his father had not been the slightest help. Except for a few ridiculous comments, he had refused to talk about what was in the letter.

"There's no need to say anything, give her the letter. After that ask her to sign for it...in front of a witness would be good...Lucy in the kitchen will do fine."

"Is that necessary? " Ronan questioned.

"I've had clients say they never received information that didn't suit them, so get her to sign."

"Am I to hand it over without any comment? Aren't you going to tell me anything? I'll look a fool if you don't," he pestered.

"There's no need for you to worry. We're all in the dark," his father said, but Ronan suspected this might be one of his famous half-truths.

"Just hand it over, for God's sake, don't make a meal of it Ronan," Sean Dalkey warned, "Really, I'm sorry I can't do this myself, but I've every confidence in you." They both smiled knowing that Sean's confidence manufactured itself when required. This sort of thing would not be up his street. He did not like tears or having to play the nanny.

Father and son were very different characters. They had grown out of different circumstances: the father's post-war frugal years, the son's 1960/70s affluent years. The father was a self-made man coming from humble beginnings. He had taken advantage of the education offered to him because he was "a bright boy"; he had worked hard and had marked out a successful but unpretentious career for himself. His attitude was as plain as his lifestyle and, although he would have been quite happy to see his son joining forces with what he considered to be the more decorative side of the population, he himself preferred to limit his contact with it.

Looking out from his office desk on to the bleak back garden, Ronan sat musing. Among the rubble, even in summer, there was nothing much to distract, except an occasional rat scampering over the stones or Mrs McHugh throwing acorns from her kitchen door for the red squirrels. Usually he was easily distracted by these little details but today none of it seemed to matter; when his thoughts wandered they quickly snapped back as if on an elastic band. Clearly he should have been forewarned about the contents of the letter. If it brought bad news Liadan might break down. Then what would he do? What if the letter told her that Maurice Agan had owed large sums of money or that her inheritance must be used to bring up hordes of his illegitimate children? Maybe Agan had written to inform her of some ghastly fact about her stepmother, Felicity, the not so-fictional evil stepmother. He groaned: that would please a lot in the town; they thought her well "above herself"; he had often heard his aunt say so; his uncle called her "a caution".

He threw a tennis ball against the wall so that it rebounded above his head and he jumped to catch it. "Of course it could be great news for her", he told himself. But he had hardly had the thought before it was rejected: no one would keep good news a secret.

* * *

"Your father's letter is sealed and confidential," Ronan said gently.

Best to let her know she would have to explain its contents if she wanted his help; he wanted to reach out to her, speak as a friend. She looked shocked.

Liadan looked so disturbed that his throat tightened. It made him more desperate to give his support, to show he understood - and yes, he felt unbearably curious. Her hand brushed her hair away from her face and she pushed her knees against the table. For a moment she looked as if she might get up and leave. He watched in horrified anticipation - had he smiled too much? Maybe he had not acted with professional ease. Slowly her questioning eyes pulled away from his and he felt at a loss: how should he proceed? She seemed brittle at times. How could he contact her through such a barrier of incomprehension? Although he was a few years older than her they had played together as children, but now how very little they understood one another. Many considered her spoilt. His father thought she would be a whole lot of trouble.

He started to speak quickly, "Mr Agan instructed us to hand this to you on your eighteenth birthday. You see he didn't know when..." Ronan stopped...

" He'd be dead..." Liadan finished for him, "anyway," she shrugged it off, "I know all that."

He held the letter towards her for a moment, but in his embarrassment his hand fell to the table, pulling the letter back just as her fingers closed on it and forcing her to snatch it. He tried to hide his discomfort, "I hope I have covered..."

"Wonderfully," she broke in sarcastically.

Forcing himself to go on, "your father wanted us to suggest that you return the letter to our safe keeping," Ronan hesitated, "I'm sorry, I have to say these things." He felt silly and she was looking at him as if she agreed with his feelings. It was all very odd. The man had written his will. So why write a letter to his daughter to be opened on her 18th birthday, Ronan wondered, when she lived with him? What could be so dreadful that she could not be told. People with a bit of property liked to make their affairs complicated. He felt confident that the letter would be about land or money, maybe even a matter he did not want Felicity Agan to know. At that thought he glanced towards the veranda. But that was it - it had to be that – there was no other explanation. "Oh bloody hell!" he thought, "What an idiot I've been". How would Liadan explain his visit to day to Mrs Agan? If only she knew she could trust him..

"Can I help in any way?" he appealed, his voice lowered. "Would you like to ask me anything?"

"I haven't read the letter yet?" she spoke severely, "and anyway I don't have any questions."

Liadan was a bit like a cornered kitten, she hissed and struck out; she was not friendly. Why was she so fearful, clawing at supposed enemies? Everyone seemed to be looking out for her; she should realize she was not alone. Why was she taking a trapped, back-against-the-wall attitude to him? Things had changed: a feeling of tension pervaded the place. The atmosphere was different from when, as a young lad, he used to accompany his father when he came to do business.

***

That afternoon driving up the avenue through the old beech trees, he had stopped on the rise of the bridge over the river Galley and looked from the grassy bank on to a flood plain, where masses of white lady's smock grew. Nearby a wren was kicking up a fuss behind a growth of white thorn covered in matted sheep's wool. The bird had been upset by him standing there, used, as it must have been, to having the bridge to itself. But he lingered, enjoying the familiarity of the place and hoping that Liadan would welcome him.

Over the bridge the avenue forked, the right branch of the fork going to the farmyard and the left, which Ronan took, running through brand-new, shiny, galvanised gates. This, Ronan realized later, was where the difference started. There were no thickets for wrens, no wild places. Here in the Rhododendron-filled parkland everything was trimmed, raked and treated; the occasional magnolia or lilac, though not manicured, were strategically placed. The house rose above it all, hardly touched by the efforts of newly planted honeysuckle vines. As Ronan stood between the stone pillars at the front door he remembered why he had loved to play here - the girls had been nice but he would have preferred to play with boys and so it had not been that. It had much more to do with the ease of the place: no adult supervision, no rules. The garden had seemed like a meadow. Rubber boots, broken benches, buckets, fishing rods; new wet mud and old dried mud covered the stone steps to the hall door. Weeds had time to seed in the gravel. No one had tried to tame the natural state of things. The hall door was flung open all summer long, and often Anna's donkey stood in the shade of the porch, or a large well-formed pile of donkey dung was there as a reminder of its recent visit. When Ronan arrived he would jump from the car and race down through the bushes to the lake, towards the voices of the children. Anna would hug him – kind, beautiful Anna.

Nothing tragic had happened then. They were the days before Felicity Agan took up permanent residence, though she had already started to be a constant visitor, he remembered.

***

As Liadan leaned over forcefully taking the letter, the poplar trees beyond the lawn shivered in a current of air. A soft breath of wind floated through the lemon trees that stood in large pots near the veranda window. The room was filled with scent. With the curtains' gentle movement the ticking of the clock seemed too slow and a restfulness settled over the room.

She turned away from him to open her letter, breaking the blood-red seal. Her hand moved up and down the paper as she began to read. Unconsciously she pushed herself deeper into the armchair, lifting her legs over the arm of it, as if somehow she could diminish herself, physically and mentally, shrinking back into her childhood. Her hand crept to her throat in a totally un-conscious gesture. She was oblivious of her young beauty. Her beauty mattered not a jot to her; to tell her she was beautiful would have caused her neither delight nor pain. Her looking-glass filled her with indifference. She was unaware that she had all the physical beauty of her sister. Later she would be grateful that she had some of the fierce and vehement passion that had so characterised Anna. Anna, the wild and the gentle, the wise and the wilful, the light of so many eyes.

***

Tuskar Rock House.
December 1979

To my daughter Liadan,

Lia, my Darling,
I have chosen to write to you in an official sort of way so that, if needs be, this letter may be used as evidence in a court of law. Also, if I were to become ill, before you've grown up, I needn't rush to tell you. I will be able to bide my time, having written this letter, knowing that all will be revealed when you are old enough to hear it.
Sean Dalkey is a good friend and a trusted solicitor. He has undertaken to hold this letter in his safe-keeping.
Don't be alarmed about what I am going to tell you. It's his-tory and none of it can harm you. In any case it's the truth and I must make sure you know the truth.
Keep this letter locked away. I know I can trust you. You will understand why when you have read it.

A forlorn look spread over her face. He had said that she need not worry too much. But her eyes stared, her heart beat faster. Her lips became dry. Of course she knew a little of what he might tell her. A person had died at the lake and though it was not her father's fault, he had been a witness and so, horribly, had she. Confused memories haunted her - shadows in her head. Like him, she suffered from nightmares. She suffered the recurring headaches of the stressed, as he had developed a recurring need to drink. Although Liadan had never developed the gruff, self-justifying nature that had been Maurice's, she had always felt that they shared a wavelength: she had known and was able to anticipate his reactions; she understood when he would go to ground or when he would stand and fight. She was able to interpret his moods and they never disconcerted her.

She knew why Maurice had spent hours in his workroom; his drinking was an open secret. The green drawers had held bottles of Power's Whiskey underneath pages upon pages of old and new drafts of the letter. He was forever rewriting. He would light a log fire and put his whiskey bottle to warm on the mantelpiece. Sometimes he locked his door, so she would not find him drinking, but mostly he forgot or was too drunk to care. Whether she was there or not he spoke aloud as he wrote; his thoughts were hardly ever coherent.

***

"The Fitzwilliams left the country," he had once started as she was sitting by the fire. "That good-for-nothing ran away .... Anna's death was his fault..."

"I'm not listening, not when you're drunk. You're disgusting... dribbling and slobbering over everything...Paddy never ran away," she snarled, "and leave Anna out of it."

He tore the pages he had written, pens flew towards the fire, his glass followed suit, causing the flames to explode into the chimney, "Get out," he shouted, "Get out."

"I'm going; don't waste your time writing a lot of rubbish – I won't read it anyway." her colour was as high as his, her anger a match.

On another day when tempers had quietened down she vexed him again, "What are you doing, Daddy?" she had peered around the door.

"I'm busy," he grumbled at her. "I've told you, I'm writing your letter Lia, go away."

He yanked the deep drawers in his desk exploding with irritation as they became stuck. "Bloody bastards," he spat out spraying saliva in his rage.

Some mischief made her say, "I was in here yesterday and had real trouble shutting them...the kittens got in...were tearing things. I just came to tell you...oh well, if you don't want to hear..." she said, trying to sound cross as he upped the volume on his swearing. Why did he have to get so mad? Could he not take a joke?

"Blast them," he fumed, "I hold you responsible, they shouldn't be in the house. I'll get that fool of a vet to put them down; I'm warning you... or I'll wring their necks myself. I'll get rid of the whole damn lot of them."

"What's the point...bloody fool," she said under her breath.

"What'd you say...come back here, Miss."

She was gone.

Mostly she let him be but occasionally, his mind off the letter, he would be incensed over some other grievance, like the new road, which he perceived as an affront to his position and rights as a landowner, and then she would rev him up some more.

"Not a chance," he would say about the proposed Templeslaney bypass. "There'll never be a road through my land; no need for it."

"They've taken "gullible" out of the English dictionary," she would say to him when contradicting had no effect. But mostly he was too drunk to answer. During those she could have read his letter a dozen times over, because, even when sober, hiding his private papers would not have occurred to him. She might come into his room unannounced, but she would never sneak around, not his little Lia. However, it was not her conscience that stopped her, only fear. The writing of the letter took the form of a ritual like the placing of a shield at an entrance, a symbolic show of protecting one's property. She would beg to be told, insist it was her right, but at the same time know the shield was in place. Every time she heard him say, "I'm writing it down; you're still too young," she would sigh with relief.

***

A tear ran down her nose; her hand brushed it away. Grasping the letter tightly she made her way over to the piano; her bare feet made no sound. She walked through the light that slipped from the embroidered curtains onto the cream carpet, washing the rosette of celandines white. Further out, where they bordered the carpet, they were a bright silky orange. Glimmering light reflected back from the gold leaf mirror. As the day crept on, the window blinds cast shadows in the corners.

As you will notice from the date on the letter, I am writing this nearly five years after Anna's death. This anniversary struck me as significant and spurred me on. I made a vow to finish this letter when I was at her grave this morning.

***

They buried Maurice with Anna. Liadan saw in her mind's eye the tombstone with silver spiky lichens. It stood alone in front of a tall hedge of yew and holly. She had fixed her eyes on the red berries when they lowered the coffin. The sun hardly ever reached Anna's grave and on that day the rain had fallen the whole time. People gathering near the grave had slipped on the saturated earth as they stepped off an overgrown gravel path, thick with tall thistles and black flax stalks - their blue heads long dead and gone. Rough, coarse grass and poppy seed-heads separated Anna's grave from the many other graves which surrounded the steps that led up to a stone cross at the centre of the graveyard. As they buried Maurice a local boy swung backwards and forwards on the little gate close by, making it screech continually. In the end it had been Ronan who had stepped forward to lift the boy from the gate.

***

"Did I tell you why we buried her in the corner of the graveyard away from the others?" Over and over, he needed to tell her. She heard his voice. Some things never change even after death, and for a moment anger welled up.

***

He would have a drink and then another. He would go on telling her.

"Our darling Anna... seventeen. We couldn't bear that she be buried with all the old people. She was our little girl. I wonder if we were wrong to put her there? She seems so alone."

"She hardly knows."

"I wonder have you many memories of her? You were small when she left."

"Of course I do." Liadan hated these conversations.

"She sparkled didn't she, dancing and singing around the house? Oh my darling girl... I remember how she loved to be a Diva... acting the maggot. Oh! Oh!" Maurice sighed. "Maria Callas through and through... Maria's gone too." He said his voice breaking "...did you know?" He rambled on swallowing his words as he drank. " I got a good ticking off!" He slurred and wept. A loud gulp followed and another glass was finished.

"Pour me another one, Lia." His voice, gradually losing its edge, grew less easy to understand but the request was as clear as air. The fire in the hearth spat out the only answer he got. Liadan hunched her shoulders and turned a page of her book.

"You could switch the light on," he whinged at her, and as she moved to do as he asked, he added, "and while you're up, a drop more Lia –*ple*ase," holding up his empty glass. "Good girl."

His mottled hand trembled, but Liadan did not look at him. She left his request hanging in the air, slamming the door as she went out.

***

Do you remember the time, my darling, before our Anna's death, the time when we drained the lake that last summer? We were down by the lake every day!

She looked into the tall mirror.

Remembering, that was all she ever did! Day after day, year after year – the house was full of memories. It was as though everything had stood still back then and anything that had happened since had just provided a context in which they could remain with her. She did not wish to leave or to tidy away the past; she liked the almost static world it created around her; she liked to inhabit it undisturbed.

CHAPTER 5

1984

There was a knock and Wendy's head appeared around the drawing-room door.

Liadan looked up from her letter and frowned. "What do you want?" she asked coldly.

There are people in this world who, no matter how rude one is to them, do not take offence and Wendy was one of these. Liadan found this one of Wendy's most irritating characteristics. Wendy, she considered, was like a stick insect, and Liadan had never liked stick insects. She was a camouflaged and inconspicuous individual, who mimicked her environment, insinuating her presence and pervading her surroundings. Even her movements triggered a shudder of annoyance.

She now crept into the room, her arms held away from her sides, her feet in the shape of a V, like a ballerina.

"Hi Ronan," she said softly, "it's been a long time." She looked too thin to be well. At seventeen she had blossomed, at twenty-seven she looked a faded thirty-five-year-old.

Liadan watched how Ronan's eyes softened. "Typical response", she thought. Her lips shut into a thin line, then tightened a bit more. People did not see Wendy as she really was; she seemed to melt something in them. Liadan could not fathom it. But then there were all those people who liked to have stick insects as pets and perhaps, she thought with a mental shrug, the explanation lay somewhere in this direction. The most aggravating of all Wendy's traits was surely that she always appeared when she was least wanted; Liadan found it totally exasperating.

They had nothing in common except Anna. And not even Anna's memory could alter the effect of Wendy's presence on Liadan. She felt stifled in her company. Wendy loved to come and stay; there was nothing that Liadan could do about it. Should she resist, Felicity would lecture "Showing good manners makes one a better person." and Lucy would huff at Liadan's lack of feeling. Everyone, including herself, would agree she was nasty to Wendy; but how could she help herself? She found Wendy excruciating, like a high-pitched scratch on a blackboard. She was fed up with saying sorry. "*Mea culpa, mea culpa, mea maxima culpa*," Liadan would mockingly whisper under her breath. Since Anna's death Wendy showed all the signs of wanting to be a martyr; she seemed to long for it. No amount of rudeness on Liadan's part had the desired effect and Liadan was always left with an angry, aggressive feeling of impotence.

To add to her sensation of discomfort, she could not deny that she would have been pleased if Ronan had looked at her in the same way as he had looked at Wendy – and not with that look of curiosity she had received from him earlier.

"We're having tea on the veranda; are you going to join us?" Wendy asked in a little voice.

"Have the papers come yet? " Liadan asked, trying not to mimic the sweetness.

"Yes, the local one..."

"Get it, will you?" Liadan asked too curtly, so she added gently, "Is there any news today?"

"What did your last maid die of?" Wendy laughed. "I think Felicity said there was something."

She went out, closing the door behind her. The paper lay on a table across the hall, hardly necessitating the closed door, but Wendy did things her way and her way always annoyed Liadan. Within seconds she was back, moving positively now that she had a purpose. Liadan took The Echo without a word, leaving Wendy standing at the piano.

"Remember this?" Wendy leant down and struck some notes. "I always remember you playing Chop Sticks...faster and faster until Maurice started to shout!" She giggled.

Ronan laughed. Both girls looked up at him, their expressions similar, their memories one memory. When recently someone had asked if they were sisters - after all they were both slim and of a similar colouring - Liadan had felt so stung that she was unable to answer. She had wondered how anyone could have made such a hideous mistake, unless it wasn't a mistake at all, and they were just being malicious!

"I'd forgotten you knew each other," she smiled at Ronan. "Be nice!" she said to herself. With a deep sigh she slid her letter back into the envelope. She opened the paper out.

"It's years since… " Ronan stopped mid-sentence.

"Nine or ten at least," Wendy said.

Liadan read aloud, ""*Updated news on the progress of the new road, Page 4.*" There should be a bit about us in here. Oh! Here we are." She folded the paper over.

"*There were angry scenes at Tuskar Rock House yesterday when Mrs Agan and Ms Liadan Agan, their family friends and neighbours demonstrated against the draining of the Estate Lake. Professor McBride, an expert on wild fauna and flora, said the ecology of the whole area would be ruined. Mrs Agan felt the house and outbuildings, unique to the area, would be undermined.*"

"This is what I said on the phone, word-for-word," Liadan explained. "Good reporting except for the angry scenes. There were so few people - hardly enough for an angry scene." She had felt disappointed at the time but not surprised. Everyone knew the road was coming. "*Fait accompli, I'm afraid darling,*" Felicity had said. Liadan sighed. "Nothing will change the direction of that road, everyone is for it anyway."

Wendy sighed too, only much more deeply, "No, they're not…I'm not, for one, Tigger."

Liadan scowled; she hated that nickname. Only Wendy called her Tigger. Everyone said it was sweet, even Anna had, and when Liadan had retaliated by calling Wendy "the Donkey, Gad's sister" everyone had ganged up on her.

"Yes they are, Wendy; that's why it's been virtually agreed. Even if the whole of the County Council voted as they said… it would still go through. You know that and I know that." Liadan's voice grew louder. She was fit to burst. "We've got to think of something or other to get the road diverted."

"Find a rare spotted something in the lake." Wendy suggested.

"Very humorous..."

"It wasn't meant to be funny, sorry!"

"No? It was really funny," Liadan simpered.

Ronan looked from one to the other.

"Well now he knows I can't stand her," Liadan thought.

***

Liadan had wanted to leave The Rock when Maurice died. To run away, let them find whatever they could find. She blamed her home for all that had happened. Refusing to campaign with her neighbours against the road, she had eagerly waited to see the house, the farm, the lake, everything demolished with all its memories. But later she had relented: Maurice's secret had to stay hidden. Besides, her home haunted her when she stayed away. Sometimes, when in Italy, she would lie in bed at night looking at the ceiling, imagining the cloudy skies of Tuskar. Then memories would flood in, floating above her like the imagined clouds. The sheen of the lake rippling in an uneven breeze. The badgers' setts above the tennis court. The hay barn swing that swung so high they could see into the swallows' nests in the rafters. Lucy and Charley she missed most of all. If she did not go home who would care for it all? Her longing had always grown into unsettling dreams and then the nightmares would begin: Tuskar derelict, surrounded by wasteland.

In the end she knew she had to go back to the big house with its windows opening onto the green lawn and tall beeches with their great arms stretching over the deep moving shadows that they cast, the long wall stretching vertically from the house almost as far as the eye could see, the rose beds now so beautifully cared for by Felicity, and the memories...; she needed it all and somehow she felt that it all needed her. Felicity never questioned her change of heart.

***

49

When Ronan spoke his voice sounded dry.

"Do you need me any longer?"

Liadan shook her head.

"Do stay," Wendy said, "I forgot, Mrs Agan asked me to invite you… we're having tea," she pressed and then, before he answered, she opened the French windows and moved from the steps on to a larger terrace were Felicity sat.

Liadan noticed her stepmother's eyes fixed upon her through the window. She looked away.

"Are you coming?" Wendy called to Ronan, while he waited by the curtains, perhaps waiting for some encouragement from Liadan, but when none came he moved to a bamboo chair beside Mrs Agan. Felicity smiled. She grasped a thin wisp of her hair, placing it high upon her regal head. When she turned to Ronan, her head positioned like a Secretary Bird's, loose strands poked out like quills. She had thick eyebrows plucked into a graceful curl above strange opaque-looking eyes. Young people found her scary. There was a tightness, an inflexibility about her.

" Ah good!" she said, "we are a very small gathering today. Freda has let us down so I am especially *pleased* you have decided to make up the numbers. It is quite *lovely* of you to spend the afternoon with us." She sighed. "The summer will be over all *too* soon, but I expect you are looking *forward* to going back?" She spoke putting great emphasize on chosen words. She was vivacious and charming. Ronan glowed; he could not think where he was meant to go back to and thought it safer not to ask.

When Ronan did not speak she tried again.

"Liadan is a *dark horse* - I can't remember her saying anything about *you*? I thought she said a *Matt Brown* was coming around - university chap, one of your *friends, perhaps*? I'm glad it's you…he sounded too much like a shade of paint."

Ronan laughed.

Wendy poured the tea. "Have a sandwich," she offered. "These are scrummy! Try one!"

Liadan stood at the French windows, looking out at them. She could make out bits of conversation and knew Felicity would question Ronan. Let him wriggle - Felicity would have fun tying him in knots.

"Must be a lot of work." Ronan nodded towards the garden.

The dense, lush lawn swallowed gallons of water each day during this unusually dry period. Sprinklers made a line running the full length to the poplar trees. A carpet of aubrietia clung to the wall, leggy and stringy, finished for the season, but hardly missed as tiny daisy-like flowers pushed through and red Valerian sprouted at ground level. Further away through the beeches a field of barley could be seen. Roses climbed above Ronan's head, their scent mingled with the lemon trees that stood in large copper pots along the terrace.

Mrs Agan sighed, "Of course it *is*," she said reproachfully. "Gardening is one long tussle," and then she seemed to forgive him, "Oh! what a *wonderful* day." Her stretched-out words seemed to mean so much more. "Last summer was *so* wet. I began to think of Italy. But of course Liadan would have none of it. *Would you* Darling?"

Liadan sat down. A light spray reached them, carried on the summer breeze as it blew through the cascading waters from a fountain close by.

"I love it here," Liadan replied. She ran her fingers through the yellow-stemmed bamboo by her side. Bees landed and took off over their heads. Drowsily she watched Ronan, as he listened attentively to Felicity.

" ...Oh yes, *how* I agree... Sweet Pea ...my *favourite* fragrance." Felicity's voice was silky-smooth; the words melted off her tongue.

Ronan drank his tea. He seemed more relaxed with Felicity in control.

"You know Felicity, Ronan used to play here as a boy? Came with his father actually and..." Wendy spoke as she offered Ronan a scone.

"Yes I did." Ronan broke in a bit breathlessly, "Loved it here."

A sparrow landed on the wall, chirping loudly before flitting away. A moment later three more appeared. Ronan threw a crumb which landed under Felicity's chair. The sparrows dived and, like scrapping urchins, pounced on the morsels. Felicity's reprimand rang out instantly.

"Ronan, *please* don't," her words shrilled as her foot kicked under her chair, scaring the birds.

Ronan could not help himself - he jumped. Liadan thought his eyes bulged a bit; she was close to laughter. Neither girl showed any surprise at Felicity's outburst.

"Sorry," he said.

"*But you mustn't*! I am rather strict about *that* sort of thing." Her voice held that lingering quality again but Ronan continued to look uneasy. "*We* don't throw our food - not even for the birds," she said as if Ronan had argued. "It encourages all sorts! We're far too close to *the farm yard*," she laughed coaxingly at him. Reconstructing the yard away from the main house would not be beyond her capabilities. She hated all animals. "We like our animals *out* in the farmyard not in the house, *even cats*!" she said looking at Liadan.

At last her attention wandered from him.

"Anything of interest in the paper, darling?" she asked and now her voice was the teeniest bit brisker.

"Just a bit about solicitors."

A startled look appeared on Ronan's face and Liadan looked a bit smug, "What is the difference between a dry cleaner and a solicitor?" she paused, "I couldn't resist this one...the cleaner pays if he loses your suit; a solicitor can lose your suit and still take you to the cleaners."

"*DarliNG!*" Felicity cried, and for a second her hair seemed a lot spikier. "Ronan is a **solicitor**...well goodness me!"

"What is the difference between a tick and a solicitor? A tick falls off when you die..."

"That's enough Liadan, *poor* Ronan."

Ronan laughed, "You haven't changed," he said looking at Liadan.

"There's a little bit in the paper about our protest too, nothing much," Liadan said, ignoring Ronan's comment. Her thoughts immediately returned to the letter, and the road. "What'll they do ...?" She spoke aloud, not meaning to.

Everyone looked at her. "What'll who do?" they asked in unison.

"Nothing, nothing, I was just thinking aloud."

"I won't let them drain the lake," she thought fiercely. "There must be some way. I've got to read the letter... I've just got to and then I'll decide. Stop panicking," she told herself. Looking up she caught Felicity watching her. Felicity's face divulged nothing; she had not questioned Liadan about Ronan's visit that day. Of course she knew about it and she enjoyed teasing Ronan because he was being so discreet. And certainly she knew about the letter- but not the contents of the letter. It was not her way to ask a direct question; she would bide her time. Whose side was Felicity on? Whose side had she ever been on? Whose side would she take when the truth came out? How much did she know and how much had she always known? What might she do in retaliation? Liadan was not sure what Maurice might have done or why he might have done it. She knew that the final years of her father's life had been filled with desperation, but she did not know whether this desperation was the result of his own acts or of those of others; she did not know in short whether he was guilty of some dreadful deed or whether he was just an old man driven crazy by grief.

CHAPTER 6

1984

"Honestly Tig, he's really nice," Wendy said.

They stood, watching Ronan's car disappear out of sight.

"Well-mannered," Felicity approved.

"He's OK." Liadan said wishing she could get away from them.

"Oh!" Wendy tapped her nose with her finger and nodded her head.

Liadan pretended not to see, "I'm going for a walk." She knew the glances they would exchange behind her back. She could not stop her head tossing in defiance. She wanted to be alone. Since the death of her sister she often sought to be alone and when her father died this need became greater. Every day she would spend a certain time considering the events of the past, trying to remember as much as she could and come to terms with them. She did not ever want to lose the feeling of a threesome that she had regarding her relationship with her sister and father. She resented any intrusion into this part of her life. Felicity, having a slightly autistic side to her nature, was not an invasive person and was never tempted to intrude.

But there was no getting rid of Wendy, who fell in behind her, catching up just before the shrubs which screened a good part of the house from the lake. Felicity never went down to the lake - not if she could help it – "*so* wet and *smelly*".

"Don't you want to read your letter?" Wendy questioned from behind.

"Finished it," Liadan lied and strode on.

Wendy must have ached to know, but at least she did not ask.

Liadan felt in a desperate hurry as she quick-marched down through the tree rhododendrons. In May these had been decked with enormous white and red blossoms, but now in August they looked a little sad, their dried-up leaves drooping in exhaustion from the sun, exposing twisted trunks to view. The young Liadan had loved to play here. It was a sanctuary from prying eyes, a stone's throw from the house, yet feeling to the child many miles away as she clambered in the undergrowth and jumped in the deep bed of ancient leaf mould.

Coming out of the bushes, the blue of the sky seemed to flow into the wide expanse of the lake beneath and turn to darker hues of blue and green. She would often stand by the Kissing Gate and gaze. Beside the gate there was an old wooden stile which had been an obstacle much loved by the children. Paddy had liked to vault the gate and the young Ronan - funny how she remembered - had often thrown himself at it again and again, skinning his knees and bruising his body until Anna had begged him to stop.

"You're such a stupid weed" Liadan would taunt.

And he would retort quite happily, "You can't do it, can you? You're a weed too."

***

Liadan hung on the gate now. What seemed like trillions of flowering montbretia burst into view: green leaves with spikes of red that shifted rhythmically with the breeze, sometimes dipping gently towards the water beyond. They had grown up through the fading primrose leaves. A worn track zigzagged its way down to the lakeside where, making a T, it swung both right and left. Near the bank, at this halfway point, stood a dilapidated boathouse and an upturned rowing boat tied to a dry wooden jetty. With time, the lake had shrunk, leaving them about five feet from the water's edge. On the opposite bank, where three giant cedars grew, a rope that had hung over the lake from the highest branch of the middle cedar, now dangled over the swamp left by the withdrawal of the lake water; its frayed edges caught on the taller yellow flag iris and rushes. Dragonflies patrolled here. An abundance of carp, crowded into the smaller area of deeper water, bobbed to catch pond skaters, disturbing the quietness of the evening.

As they moved to the water's edge Liadan thought, not of the lake's inevitable demise, but of times gone by when they had gone there with their friends and sat on the landing area, dangling their feet over the water before jumping in. Now, just as then, the distinct smell of lake water and green plants filled the air. She bent down and splashed the water on to her arms. She could almost taste the lake and it brought back an intense feeling of childhood happiness. After a day of play in the water the smell had always lingered on her skin, more noticeable at bed time as she placed her head upon her arm to sleep.

They turned and walked from the landing area towards the underground shelter. Although the main path swung away from the shelter's entrance, another led straight to it, through brambles and bushes; it was still easy to push a way through, even after all the years of disuse. Back in those days it would have been impossible to walk by without noticing the buildings. Now a stranger would only see white thorn mixed with Cupressus Leylandii and glimpses of a rather rocky mound appearing above the bushes.

The shelter had been built during the latter part of the Second World War by Liadan's grandfather. "In case of a bomb attack", he had said; and in Maurice's time additions had been made. Maurice had built showers, and behind the showers an old-fashioned kitchen, with wheel-controlled bellows for an open fire. A stone corridor led the way to the shelter entrance. Grandfather Agan's lead-lined water tanks supplied clean water. That was then – now it was all just a bad memory since Anna's death. She had left her shoes outside the kitchen door that dreadful day. After that it must have been Maurice who had nailed up signs warning of danger and had circled the buildings with barbed wire.

On a whim the two girls pressed forward, ignoring the prickly shrubs and carefully avoiding the wire, just to have a look. Smiles of remembrance accompanied their quickening heart beats. Neither girl had been there for years. There were grass tufts and sphagnum moss on the window-sill of the shower-room and the floor was criss-crossed with the silver trails of slugs. On the back wall of the shower-room hung ceramic decorative plaques of fat men running; the largest was to the left and each decreased by a third, in a take-off of the three ubiquitous china mallard ducks in flight. They could both remember when Maurice had hung them on the wall.

"Don't tell Felicity, she'd think them vulgar!" He grinned.

***

Liadan missed him dreadfully. She even missed the broken man he had become at the end. She felt now that if only he were alive, she would insist that he tell her everything; it had been a bit like a game of cat and mouse: she had teased him and he had tried to evade all confrontation.

Her mind returned to the letter. She thought she knew who had died; he would have been dropped in at the northern side of the lake where they never swam. Then after Anna, what did any of it matter? There would be nothing earth-shattering anyhow; her father blustered but he was never a killer. Still that letter threatened her, looming, as it did in her mind, like a giant cobweb. Once she had read it – then she would be free.

"Obviously that poor fellow's death was a dreadful thing," she said to herself, as if someone were listening in to her thoughts and accusing her of callousness. All this going over things, thinking and thinking would drive her mad. She was so bored with her own thoughts. How she hoped he would leave Anna out of the letter. She had her own feelings to contend with and she did not need his pain as well. Besides, Anna would always be there; it was not as if Liadan could ever forget her.

She pulled at her lips. One remembered incident worried her greatly – but surely it would turn out to be untrue. About two months after Anna's funeral, while in Italy, where they had all gone after Anna's death, she had overheard a conversation between Maurice and Felicity.

"You're not innocent in all of this," Felicity had said.

And Liadan had felt cold inside; she had not dared to inter-vene, to make her presence known. How could Maurice not be innocent, he adored Anna? What did it mean? Felicity could be downright scary. She should have rushed to the defence of her father; she should never have stayed quiet but she had put her head down and placed cushions over her ears.

**

When they reached the cedar trees Wendy dropped like a stone on to the bank, her legs splayed out on the grass, looking like a helpless giraffe. She lay back and moaned with pleasure at the beauty of the evening.

The light on the lake dwindled and the shadow from the trees grew long, reaching out towards the centre of the water as the day came to a close. On the opposite bank the wooden jetty seemed to be circled by a mist where the cottongrass had gone to seed. The singing of the birds in the quiet of the evening seemed louder. Close by a moor hen circled her chicks, trying to gather them close to her. The sky started to fill with yellow light from the house. The high-pitched calls of circling bats were no longer audible to Liadan but she strained her ears in an effort to hear them, her mind floating back to the sounds she had heard as a child.

1974

He ran to the water's edge, only to stand and stare at the cold lake until they started to chant.

"Ronan jump," they chanted, "Jump! Jump! Jump!" Eventu-ally he had to.

And then he did, but as his feet hit the water they heard him call, "Can't swim!". Shocked they jumped into the lake, clothes and all, frantically searching, but he had gone. "The Brat", as Liadan called him then, finally popped up by the cedar tree rope. He was laughing at their wet clothes and frightened faces.

Often when Wendy arrived Anna would leave hurriedly and swim to the jetty to greet her. Liadan hated Wendy; she always ruined everything, dragging Anna away often far up towards the northern side of the lake where no one could hear them. That was the picture that remained: the two girls sitting in the boat, oars resting on their knees, heads close together exchanging secrets. Liadan would have to wait and wait for their return before the playing could restart.

Others might arrive and leave but the games went on all day. Boat battles, rounders, French cricket... anything and everything. They squabbled over scores and gamesmanship. When someone hit the ball out of bounds an excursion back to the lakeside took place. This might lead to sporadic bathing. Sometimes Anna made pancakes in the kitchen by the lake. For short periods Liadan's friends were allowed to turn the wheel of the bellows, but in the end they were excluded. Liadan suspected Anna's group liked the pancake-making best because, in the crowded little kitchen, they could chat, tell secrets and make it impossible for the younger group to stay and listen in on their talk. In a huff Liadan would lead the younger ones away. With her finger on her lips she would open the door and they would move hesitantly down the narrow passageway of the air-raid shelter which led to the older rooms built by the girls' grandfather. Often the thrill of the dark passage and the children huddling along it would be too much and would erupt into what was almost hysteria. Opening the door the cold air and darkness would engulf them like a presence and they would wait for Anna's entreaties to return to the safety and heat of the fire. Weird echoes would chase them back.

"There was something in there," they would shout close to hysteria, "something trapped."

One day Ronan Dalkey, perhaps wishing to impress, pushed the game a little further with his boastful remarks.

"It's better than playing Dungeons and Dragons." Ronan had said to Liadan as they found themselves in the dark passageway. "I can go right in if you like," he offered. "I'll tell you what's there if you're scared."

"I'm not scared, smarty," Liadan protested. "Anyway I know what's there."

He looked at her in disbelief, then went ahead and she had to follow.

Ronan Dalkey's parents were spending the day with Maurice and Felicity and she would have to put up with him for the whole day. "I'm never having him to play again." she thought. "Never..." He did not look the sort of boy that would be brave. He was small for a 12-year-old, with black curly hair that grew more vigorously than he himself did. His thick-rimmed glasses helped to hide his podgy face, and Liadan thought him squidgy - not nice to touch; a brainy boy too - the sort who challenged her too much.

The outer door swung back and forth behind them and a gentle warm breeze followed, mingling with the cold dank air that took over as they crept along the passageway. An uneven floor and the darkness made it difficult to keep a steady course; they slid their hands along the cold and slimy wall, feeling into crevices and touching a world of wet and shapeless things. Liadan kept going, her feeling of dread growing until her only recourse was to stuff her fist into her mouth to stop her screams. Her heart throbbed in her throat. In the heavy air each breath was short and panicked. Supposing the roof fell in? She could too easily visualize herself being buried alive and, why, of all the people in the world, did it have to be with him?

At the end of the passageway she could sense the door was open into the first room. Ronan had moved further from her and she missed his warmth and lost his shape in the complete blackness. She remembered someone told her that bats had been shut in and their ghosts hung from the rafters. Any minute she expected the slap of a wing against her head and she cried out when her face became engulfed in spider webs. There were lots of entrapped bodies in the webs; she could feel the lumpy masses in her hair.

She had seen the tiny bundles in the webs on earlier visits with her grandfather; she knew the room and the low-ceilinged area beyond, where anything could be hiding. Her grandfather had always held her hand and she had gripped so tightly that he groaned in protest, making her laugh. In his other hand he would hold a torch scattering the light around the room. "We've got kerosene lamps, tins of fruit and vegetables and bins of everything you can think of, even soap," he would say proudly. He told Liadan he would bring down all her favourite books; then he would name all his favourite children's books, particularly the one he loved the best: Gulliver's Travels. "Not Gulliver's Travels, what about Yakari, I want all the books about Yakari." Liadan had been insistent. The lists had seemed important, but now she had no time for lists. If only she could get out alive she would never play this stupid game again. Everyone would be angry if they found out. It was out of bounds.

"Let's go back?" she whispered.

"Let's look around the room; you're not scared are you?" His voice boomed.

"We can't see, what's the point?" She tried to keep her voice steady as she whispered back to him. She couldn't care less about the little twit or what he thought of her anymore. "There's nothing here. We're not meant to be here... Daddy said. I'm going back," again her voice was low, but an edge had crept into it. She wanted him to go back with her but nothing would have made her ask.

"OK," he said so loud she ached to kick him. In this small space why did he have to shout? Instinctively she kept her voice low - in case - but how could she explain to him? She hated him.

When they turned to go back she found herself behind him. He had led her in and now he was leading her out. With her back turned to the empty space and the darkness, a shudder ran through her like an electric shock. She could almost feel a presence walking behind her. "Oh please, oh please," she whispered under her breath, "I'll never come back here if only I can get out this time." When she had closed the door at the end of the corridor she had vowed that Ronan Dalkey would suffer.

Ronan had never been made to suffer. He had remained unaware of Liadan's feelings, partially because, even as a child, he had always been a participator rather than an observer and he had never guessed how she felt about him. He did not look for explanations for her caustic remarks, taking them often just as a sign of her wit and incision. It was true that she was often blunt where others would have been more conciliatory, but most people felt that, given the events in her life, it was not extraordinary she should show a certain amount of scepticism.

1984

He hadn't improved, Liadan decided, and then she smiled to herself, because so obviously he had.

"He's got a younger sister, hasn't he?" Liadan asked.

Wendy started. She had been chatting away, complaining no doubt about office life, her favourite topic. It was obvious she had not heard Liadan and she went on after a moment's hesitation.

"Just gossip... unbelievable." Her eyebrow shot to her hairline.

Talking when no one listened - Liadan shrugged her shoulders - that's unbelievable.

"People will say anything..." Wendy repeated again as if a recap had been requested. "The Fitzwilliams can't be selling up, I don't believe it - do you? I was really looking forward to seeing Paddy again."

Liadan sat up, she was listening now. "No, they can't be."

"Actually that's what I said, but Moira insisted, she said she'd heard."

"But don't they know...*don't they know that if they give up we haven't got a chance.*"

"Oh it's probably not true." Wendy drew a long breath and in a soothing voice she sighed "You know how they are in the office."

"In that case why go on about it." Liadan felt frightened.

"It's talk." Wendy explained. "I told you, it probably isn't true."

Liadan stared back. She wanted to blame Wendy for this news. She turned away to let Wendy's words drift past, but Wendy went on talking. Why did she have to say things that she knew would be upsetting? ... so typical of Wendy! *Why had Anna liked her?* She asked herself this question nearly every day.

If the Fitzwilliams sold it would be the end. Their opposition to the road had been crucial; the two families fighting side-by-side had a chance. She could almost accept the loss of the lake, but the fear of what would be found she had not the fortitude to face alone, not without the promise of Paddy's support. Now it was imperative that she was not left in ignorance, not a moment should be lost.

Chapter 7

1984

*O*f course you remember a little of what happened that day. I have tried not to bring back bad memories, but just to sketch out for you the necessary details of what really took place. Before, I did everything in my power to stop you remembering. I wanted you to hold on to your childhood. I tried to pretend nothing major had happened and this would have worked if only Anna had heeded me. No matter what, I could not make her see that everything would be all right.

Yes, he had tried everything to stop her remembering, and not for the first time she felt it was the cause of her recurring nightmares. Anna had been older and so more difficult to persuade: she would not have easily accepted an ambiguous situation. Liadan could remember her clear blue eyes and her candid incomprehension of any necessity for subterfuge at any time. The case of Liadan had been different: she had simply been too young for any real understanding of what had or had not taken place. She had done her best to suppress memories, to believe her father and to acquiesce in his desire that she should forget.

Maurice would stand by her bed, cup in hand, ready with the hot, sweet-tasting drink on those evenings when she had become distressed. Mostly her memories were very confused, but if ever they had threatened to become less clouded he made sure to distract her from them; she could see that now.

One such early November night a storm had blown up and quickly strengthened to a forceful intensity driving the raindrops against the windows, howling at the stricken beeches, cracking the thin young branches as it rushed through them. Her cosy bedroom insulated from most winter nights could not hold this storm completely at bay. She could hear a cow calling for its calf during the lulls of the angry wind. It seemed to her as if people were crying out, were calling to her and telling her about the lake. Someone seemed to say, "They are all dying."

"Who are?" Maurice knelt down by his daughter's bed.

"No one will tell me Daddy."

"Drink a little; it's a dream," he took her hand; he kissed her forehead, "You are my brave little Lia."

The curtains with their mad dashes of bright yellow and reds were tightly drawn against the night. Above her bookcase was a Swiss clock with long chains reaching down to a framed picture of the family. The clock had stopped years before - the cuckoo's head was stuck out as though ready to sing, its wings expanded in imaginary flight. When she was alone the cuckoo seemed to speak to her and sometimes it sounded a lot like her father. On either side of her bed were pictures of angels holding white lilies. Liadan liked to talk to them when the cuckoo said too much.

"You were shouting, 'bloody bastard'."

"Lia, bold girl!" her father cried, "Daddy never said such a bad word."

But Liadan had wondered: she knew he used lots of bad words. He would lean over her and rearrange her bedding, tucking her in tightly until she giggled. And he would always continue to deny everything.

"Silly! Daddy would never do such a thing."

"Lia, my darling, Daddy wouldn't say such a thing."

"Why did they bring dogs to the lake, Daddy?" Liadan would ask as she sipped.

"Dogs are good sniffers." Maurice would wrinkle his nose and do an imitation of a dog sniffing her pillow. She would squeal in delight. "I think I can smell some sweets hidden here. You're spilling your drink silly!" He would take the cup from her hands.

Liadan tried to forget her dreams of dead people by the lake; she wanted to believe what Lucy had said.

"Stuff and nonsense, that's all it is. They got a tip-off, love."

Liadan hadn't known what that meant and asked.

"Gossip in the town." Lucy had said, snapping the heads off young carrots with her strong fingers. "Superintendent Furlong came…remember? He said his men would have to search the area. Silly man, that's all I'll say. Don't go on, love." She said to Liadan's pleading, "Of course they found nothing. What did they expect - silly men! Nothing to do with you, all this."

***

The giddy dogs ran up and down by the brindle shore. As their noses found different scents they veered away from the lake edge, back along the path and further on to the ravine, but each time, on Superintendent Furlong's instruction, Garda Brady brought them back to start all over again. Maurice stood with the men, his eyes cold, his mouth smiling.

"I did a spot of beagling in my younger days, I'd be surprised if your dogs found anything here," he said.

When eventually they came upon the shelter, the dogs had to be called to heel, eager as they were to move on they could hardly be restrained long enough to give a cursory snuffle around the showers and a swift sniff at the old entrance. There was a dark stain left from a spill of Jeyes Fluid at the entrance, and the smell that was no longer detectable to the human nose was still evident to the hounds, and they did not like it. Encouragement from Maurice to enter the shelter persuaded Garda Brady to move timidly down the passageway for a quick look into the dark rooms beyond. Dead leaves, old twigs and the general smell of dank decay gave them enough excuse to look elsewhere. And when Felicity appeared full of admiration for their recklessness, their minds were made up.

"I hope you've told them it's at their own risk, Maurice. No one goes there, it's *too* dangerous." She spoke to Maurice but her eyes were on Superintendent Furlong. "I thought you said the ceiling was sagging, didn't a *slight* indent appear in the mound three months ago? Poor innocent hounds…so *brave*!" She turned away. "It's all very well but you'll be the one who'll be blamed." Her voice became low and Maurice noticed how the policemen strained to hear what she said.

Maurice laughed a little hysterically ... and said to the Superintendent, "Felicity is helping me refurbish the house."

* * *

"Let's read a little before you go to sleep," Maurice said to Liadan but she shook her head, much more interested in the activities of the dogs.

"What were they sniffing for at the lake?" She asked

"Maybe a ..." he said, "or a..."

"A rifle?" Something seemed to dawn in her flushed expression; a look of anxiety followed, deepening in her large round eyes.

"Nonsense.... they were looking for a pen," he hesitated. "Paddy lost his father's pen when he fell in the lake, don't you remember? After they had gone home, Tom rang to ask me to find it." The words tumbled out.

"A pen!" Liadan exclaimed, "But Paddy was crying! Why did he cry? I don't remember that." Watermark traces of light yellow on her forehead had replaced the dark purple of bruising visible before. Maurice leant forward and stroked her hair, making curls around her ears.

"You don't remember because you fell over and hit your head, poor darling. That gold pen cost a lot of money and Tom wanted us to look for it," he told her. "Anyway, Paddy's such a poodle," he tickled her a little, "or a little soft r- r- rabbit," he whispered into her ear. She giggled with delight.

"I'm going to tell him, I am," she said.

"No, no!" he begged her in mock horror and she giggled some more.

"When is Paddy coming back?"

"Have another sip, Lia."

"I miss him."

She sat drinking as he had ordered her to do, lifting the glass high over her head to drain the last drop. A feeling of inevitability washed over her; memories were foggy, images and shapes, a spectral shade appearing and then gone. Cows, the cuckoo clock and the crying wind were all silenced.

"Anna keeps asking me what happened but I can't remember." Liadan said. She pulled her quilt to just below her chin; she yawned, her eyes closed and she was asleep before he could answer.

He kept insisting that nothing had happened; gradually she thought nothing much had.

***

1984

Now if you do remember something of what happened you will probably wonder if there is a body buried by the lake. Let me try to explain.

She could hear him speaking. In this letter, he must be telling the truth. Something switched in her head making her feel certain: "I don't want to wonder about it all any more." she thought. She must believe the letter because surely he would not lie to her now knowing, as he almost certainly did, that he might be speaking from the grave.

She had always felt safe with her father, trusting him completely in things that concerned herself, but she knew also and, even as a child she had been aware, that often his dealings with others were complicated by his blustering nature, his strong temper and frequently overbearing manner. He was a simple and often turbulent man, but his love of his children was deep and clear and had surrounded their childhood.

Looking down at the letter Liadan suddenly had a flash of memory. "I looked down to the outlet where the water drained away and then I stood up," she said to herself. Paddy had run through the water splashing and shouting a lot - something about Anna. He was shouting, "I hate you."

"Grow up," Tom shouted back, "you're a baby."

Liadan heard her father make a sort of howling, grinding noise.

"You fool ...this is how men are," Tom sneered at them. "You're boys playing about in the water."

Definitely Liadan could remember Tom saying, "This is how men are." "Men are how?" she had wondered. She felt insulted on Paddy's behalf; Tom was Paddy's father; how could he be so mean?

Then Maurice and Tom were fighting.

Paddy's running feet slapped through the water and Liadan heard the blunted sound of punches landing and then a noise like a stake being driven into the ground.

Her father shouted.

"Get off... bastard..." The words were punctuated by loud thumping sounds.

Then there was nothing more except a roaring sound in her head.

***

All the mischief started when the Fitzwilliams came to the area. I don't know why but without apparent reason we were enemies from the start. I am not taking all the blame nor do I want to accuse Tom completely. I might say it was because of this or that, a straight-forward explanation; but even writing with hindsight I am unable to find a satisfactory answer. I tried to be friends with them for Felicity's sake.

On our first-ever meeting Tom and I almost literally circled each other like two dogs squaring up for a fight.

I had lived here all my life and my father before me. The sale of the farm next door could be expected to bring a different type of landowner to the neighbourhood, even one inexperienced in country ways. Tom Fitzwilliam had a lot of money but I had dealt with stockbroker types before. I heard he'd started his life in finance and having made suf-

ficient money, bought the land with the intention of doing organic farming, believing that a great deal of money could be had from the middle classes' **recently acquired interest in healthy eating,** if they were encouraged in the right way. Needless to say Tom's way was the right way.

Almost at our first meeting Tom wanted to know the state of the River Galley; was it pesticide-free? How should I know? He said that I was responsible for our Blue Stream, as you girls call it, because it springs in the Upper Water Field. He never bothered the Donovans or the Cruises, as far as I know, though the River Galley runs smack through the middle of their land. He was always bleating about too much or too little water from the lake. Could I help if it was less in summer? God forbid that there should be any pollutants in the river because Tom held me responsible.

There was no settling-in period before the requests came thick and fast for the changes Tom wanted me to make. He phoned, he stopped me in the street, accosted me in my local pub, everywhere, every day. I hated his pushiness, his businessman-like ways and his total disregard for anything I might say.

At first I tried to be reasonable but his patronizing tone and the slavish attitude of my old friends and neighbours to him just put my back up. I couldn't allow myself to do his bidding. Felicity accused me of pig-headedness, of doing the opposite of what he wanted. I admit that I do remember not clearing a ditch because he asked me to. I remember savagely cutting back a hedge that he wanted to grow. But otherwise I think I behaved pretty reasonably. Nevertheless, I felt that I had been blamed for a lot more of the discord between us than I was responsible for. Of course Jane Fitzwilliam was Felicity's friend and Paddy worked for us, so we couldn't just agree to differ. There didn't seem to be any civilized way in which Tom and I could stop meeting each other. And as "civilized" people we were forced to communicate in a false and artificial way, pretending friendship where there was none and concealing *an ever-increasing antagonism, which in the very end got out of hand.*

CHAPTER 8

1980

The town was slowly coming to life; shadows played like happy children over the houses and streets as the sun came and went. The warmth of the early autumn day was relaxing and the few people who had appeared in the streets were in no hurry to go about their business: they stopped to talk and wish each other well.

"Good morning Superintendent! Morning Mooress!" Tom shouted across the square.

The exuberance of the man felt like a low heavy cloud bearing down on Maurice. Tom looked healthy; his skin was dark from foreign travel. He had mischievous eyes, a sardonic smile; so excessively good looking and he was a popular man.

"Great day… lovely weather lads." Tom made his way towards them.

Maurice would have liked not to notice him but that was not possible with Tom. He stood at the door of Seals pub talking with Harry Furlong; a minute later he might have missed the encounter, but such was his luck.

"Good morning, Tom," he answered reluctantly.

Harry waved in an offhand manner. Maurice envied Harry his ease - but then Maurice could never be himself with Tom.

"The beech Mooress, the beech, any chance of lopping that branch?"

Mispronouncing his name always had the desired effect and Maurice scowled, "Not a chance today I'm afraid Tom …want to catch Mick in here… order the harvester. The wheat heads have dropped…"

"Does that mean it's ready to cut?" Harry asked.

Maurice nodded. "Just a bit of a late crop… still, it needs cutting." Maurice did his best to ignore Tom. "I hear you're over in Bunclody at the moment, Harry. How's it going?"

"How's the lovely Felicity," Tom butted in. He had crossed over to them making slow progress as he greeted many of the passers-by. The sardonic smile was there to tease Maurice and when he arrived Maurice felt teased.

"Very well, thank you." Maurice answered stiffly.

"Just a minute Tom," Harry pushed in. "Yes, we've a nasty case going on in Bunclody, but I need to have a word with you, Maurice." He spoke with authority, but without any slight being intended to Tom.

Tom laughed "Certainly," and he went on his way.

Without waiting Maurice threw the pub door open forcing the Superintendent through. He was jubilant; Harry Furlong had the measure of the man. And Maurice felt satisfied he had acted with ease and not agreed to anything.

The Superintendent stood just inside the door. "I do need to have a quick word Maurice, if you don't mind."

"Of course not, fire away; you'll have a glass anyway?" Maurice tried to manoeuvre him up to the bar.

"It's about the meeting on Saturday." Harry shook his head. "No, no nothing to drink; I only came in to get out of the way."

Maurice smiled and nodded.

"There's been a lot of bad feeling about the road and I wanted to know how many you're expecting at the Show Ground. You'll be having a word I hear."

"I'm representing the farmers who might be involved, but there's nothing to worry about really, can't see it happening ... it'd take my lake and I'm not having that!" Maurice laughed. "Some fool from Dublin thinks what works in the city works in the countryside; planners my foot... Should be a good few there but nothing to worry about."

"Are ye having a drink, Mister Agan, Superintendent?" A voice rang out from the dark recesses.

Both men made a speedy retreat out into the clear cloudless day.

When Harry left, Maurice decided he might as well go home. Templeslaney was buzzing with the likes of Tom and that old drunken scrounger in Seals. He strode off down Slaney Street and was passing The Cotton Tree Café when Sylvia's head shot out. Suddenly all his good feelings were sucked out of him; yesterday in Dublin he had met her by chance.

***

"I've met everyone from Templeslaney today... might as well have stayed at home," she trilled at him. They had met on Grafton Street.

"Fancy that..." he had said, not interested. He wanted to catch the last train back that evening and after he had completed all his business buy something special for Felicity in Brown Thomas; already the best of the afternoon had flown - rotten luck bumping into Templeslaney's very own gossip-monger.

"Sylvia...I'll have to rush ...I'm late already," Maurice answered vaguely, walking away even as he saw that she had started to tell him something.

"...Felicity and Tom...suspicious me!" There were peals of laughter.

Maurice whipped around. "What" he shouted rudely.

"Oh never mind...go on...you'll miss them."

He knew straight away what she had meant, but he was not going to meet Felicity and Tom. He had thought Felicity was in Cork.

***

There had been so many occasions when he had felt equally deceived but too afraid to challenge Felicity. He thought back to 1974 when he had first asked Felicity to marry him after a succession of misunderstandings, but she had declined thinking it too soon. She had moved into Tuskar House a year earlier "to help," claiming a suite of rooms on the second floor. They had agreed to take things much more slowly.

Before Felicity moved in Maurice felt free to tell the household what he thought of Tom.

"The man's a sneering swine, a big, fat, affluent arsehole," he would rant, fuming as he marched up and down the hallway, kicking at the skirting boards, "bastard...swine." He would seem out of control but in reality he was just being Maurice. With Felicity in residence he now had to dampen down these scenes, but sometimes when something else had nettled him, and this might even have been Felicity herself, he would give vent to his feelings, while she would remain serene, her face expressionless.

"I find him rather interesting."

Interesting! It was unbearable for Maurice. He was a man who, though very much in need of the company of women, was unused to their ways and had always felt a little adrift with them. He had met Felicity through the Fitzwilliams and therefore should not have been surprised by her obvious ease with them. She had known them before she had met him; her friendship with them went back a long way. It was partially this past that they shared and of which he was ignorant that made it difficult for him. His jealousy, and he knew that was what it was, was based on a feeling of being an outsider. He could not put his finger on any actual sign or symptom which might have caused his distrust but he was never sure how much he knew and how much he did not know. It made everything so much more difficult because he felt guilty about his misgivings and yet he was unable to banish them. He hated Tom's popularity; he longed for his exposure but it did not happen. Time went by and Tom remained well-liked, sought-after and approved of. Because they were unaware of his deep dislike for the man, people continued to enthuse about Tom to him:

"You know, Tom thinks we should open a stables! Tom suggested putting our money in a pension fund! Tom's ideas about farming are so interesting..." Almost every time he met someone they seemed to want to talk about Tom and then Paddy, Tom's son, was with them every day, hired to work on the lake at the insistence of Maurice's own family.

***

"Oh please Daddy, Paddy wants a summer job and we need help; you said so," Anna begged.

"Well yes, I do need help, but not a schoolboy," Maurice told her. Benevolently he looked at his daughter but his heart felt tight. Having to have that boy about the place every day reminding him of Tom - he could not do it even for her.

"I'll help too. Oh ple*ase*... Felicity tell him," Liadan put in.

Dot and Fergus Dunn were over to dinner when Anna came to beg Maurice. Fergus Dunn thought it a grand idea.

"Such an agreeable family," Dot helped.

"Employ him yourself, " Maurice snapped back, but the hostility in Felicity's face made him add hurriedly.

"Well all right." He felt trapped.

Felicity seemed to be unaware of his sacrifice. Maurice didn't try to hide it but still she did not see. "They were so new together, how could she understand?" he kept saying to himself. In the evenings after dinner they sat close together on the veranda sipping coffee and looking out over the lawn and every evening he realised how lucky he was to be able to spend time with this gracious woman - if only one day she would agree to become permanent in his life.

Even Tom's wife inflicted wounds on Maurice's delicate ego and he could not understand this and neither could he talk about it to anyone, least of all Felicity. Though Maurice found Jane a forbidding woman he would have liked to flirt a little in friendship and bonhomie. His good nature could have been encouraged if Jane had tried. He offered his friendship and support to her when they first arrived in the district and she coldly ignored it. Something less than a smile hovered on her dark mauve-coloured lips and the rigid muscles around her mouth formed no words of greeting, no happy response. There were no neighbourly gestures of a bag of apples or a bottle of wine and any that politeness prompted her to make were limited to the bare minimum. He felt that her conduct had a certain import and that she shared this awareness: things were not equal.

Felicity, charmingly attentive when Tom appeared, was in stark contrast to Maurice. He would have liked Felicity to be a little less enthusiastic. If Jane did not find Maurice worth more than cold indifference, then cold indifference should have been Tom's lot also. Jane's purple nails scratched beneath her watch strap, happy to have found a more interesting occupation than shaking his hand.

Progressively his tongue got the better of him. People started to find it amusing; some even tried to bait him by bringing up Tom's latest achievements, hinting at future successes; until one evening in Seals pub he told them, wishing all to hear, his voice heavy with drink.

"I'd pay to see the bastard shot."

1984

Over a period of two summers Paddy came to work for me, and it just so happened the majority of his time he worked on or near the lake. This work was carried out year-in, year-out to clear the mud and dead vegetation. Attending to the bank and spreading a couple of layers of pebbles over the bottom were all essential maintenance, especially as you girls and your friends liked to swim there. This particular year I had started early because of a persistent leak. Some days into the job, Tom arrived unannounced, uninvited. He stood on the bank opposite the air-raid shelter shouting orders at me. His face, so used to smiling on the world, looked tense. In retrospect I would say he appeared tired and ill.

He sent Paddy away and strode about as if he were the master. Paddy of course went without a word, he had been working hard most of the day. Anna had arrived back at the house and I expect he wanted to see her. I knew when he left Tom would stop ferreting about. Paddy had tried to warn me about his father. He had hinted that his father liked to get a rise out of me: "All a bit of sport to him," Paddy had said. And I in turn

*understood that they, Tom and Paddy, did not get on. As soon
as Paddy left he spoke.*

*"My dear Moreess, you really must curtail your activities
right now. I must insist you stop immediately." The pompous
fool! Of course he never spoke to anyone else like this, only to
me. He wanted to rile me. The exchange that follows is almost
verbatim. I remember every word said and I am putting it here
so that you may have a better understanding of the antago-
nisms between us. I kept my cool though, you know.*

"Why?" I asked civilly. "I'm not finished."

*"You know my pump is put under enormous strain because
of your shenanigans here. I dare say you can now mend the
dam without further water loss, in fact, you can plug it here."
This curt rudeness was accompanied by the gesture of prod-
ding the dam with his stick. Even an unsatisfactory employee
could have expected more respect than he gave to me.*

He strode about proprietarily, exasperating and provoking me.

*"I must get back; we are entertaining tonight," He told me,
"I can't waste any more time on this," and his face broke into
a huge smile, a smile he had practised in a mirror no doubt.
"So many of our good neighbours have been able to come!" he
continued.*

*A not-so subtle snub - we had not been invited. Of course I
worried for Felicity, not for me, I certainly did not care.*

*Later from the dining-room window I watched you playing
with Paddy. Poor Paddy, I have heard that he has become a
recluse and is unable to find any purpose in life.*

1974

Maurice walked up and down the path by the house not calm
enough to eat. Nearing the dining-room window he could hear
Liadan's voice and the dishes being moved about. He had to
have his thinking time, he heard Felicity explain to the girls. She
always knew what to say. Soon she would have the table cleared
and out she would go into the garden, composed and perhaps a

little too aloof. Repeatedly he had asked her to marry him and eventually she had agreed, but not yet, she had kept saying, she had been so sweet. He would not allow a stray thought against her, no matter what.

That Tom! Maurice had never before come in contact with a man who aggravated him as much as Tom did. Even when Tom took to complimenting the girls Maurice's heart did not soften. He would so gladly listen to their praise all day, every day, but not when Tom decided to add his voice to the chorus. Anyone could see how beautiful Anna was; she did not need Tom to tell her.

Sometimes it was Tom's uncivil and discourteous behaviour that irritated most. That afternoon he had deliberately let Maurice know that he and his wife were entertaining the "neighbours" and that he and his family were not invited. Three weeks previously Felicity and Maurice had entertained lavishly, inviting the Donovans, the O'Connors, the Creuses and of course Tom and Jane. Tom's sneering face was still before him. A telling retort would have salvaged some of his pride and he wished with all his heart that he had ordered Tom off his land, never to set foot on it again. Why could he not have just shrugged his shoulders and said:

"I hope the neighbours enjoy their evening," and laughed like Tom would have done.

Maurice always came out of any contact with Tom deeply humiliated. He was no less intelligent than his neighbour but he was a good deal straighter and less manipulative. His reactions to the provocation that he constantly suffered were hamstrung by his desire not to involve Felicity in any unpleasantness. And she, either because of her ability to keep an emotional distance or because for some reason she was biased in Tom and Jane's favour, would certainly have seen no reason for such unpleasantness. Maurice's regard for Felicity went side by side with a desire not to invite either her displeasure or the sharper side of her tongue. Keeping cool would have made it easier to keep up a pretence of neighbourliness. Since he could not directly fall out with Tom, he should have tried to play his game.

"Now look here Tom, what's the problem?" he should have said, "I need to empty the lake to rebuild the dam; it's leaking. Rotten luck about your pump. Should be able to get the damn thing fixed! Let's have that drink?"

If only... But he could not play the game of a low-down womaniser. Next time he would punch him; that would even-up the score.

From the dining-room came the music of *Norma*. Maurice's favourite aria moved him and tears came to his eyes as the soprano sang *Casa Diva*. The music wafting about him seemed like heaven sent on warm tranquil air. The garden danced before his eyes through the rainbows of countless water sprinklers. Nearby Felicity's water fountain spouted and gurgled..

Early mornings brought him face to face with all he wanted to accomplish; his days were filled with the carrying out of these plans. By evening he often felt he had achieved so much. He smiled to himself now and laughter from his daughters brought further smiles. The music swelled up drawing him to the deserted dining-room still heavy with the rich smell of potted pheasant. He opened a bottle of Rioja and drank deeply before seating himself at the head of the table. Reflections from the white china dishes lit the mahogany wood and were further reflected in a glass display cabinet beyond. Pictures of Dutch women in the style of Vermeer, their bodies richly clad in satins, hung on the walls. Maurice remembered his light-hearted teasing of Felicity with his claims that he preferred Van Herbert to Vermeer.

"Not that argument again." she had begged. " Van Herbert is just a copyist"

And he had answered. "Yes but the picture, the end product, is painted with new paints and more advanced understanding of light etc. Originals are overrated."

She had looked at Tom then with eyebrows slightly raised. Oh, he had been there, Maurice remembered; a frown appeared on his forehead. "Forget all that!" he thought, and gazed at the chandelier hung low over the table reflecting light on the two regal, green vases beneath.

Lucy opened the hatch.

"Are you ready?" she asked, as she pushed through a steaming dish followed by his warmed plate. To Lucy it was a question of ready or not because she did not linger to hear his answer.

As Maurice ate alone, his family, although dispersed, were nearby. Hearing their voices he felt content. He thought of how he would behave if Tom appeared at the lake again: he would be in control. If Tom could not mind his manners, well then, he nodded his head. "Sorry Felicity!" he would say "I did my best." Paddy would be away at the end of the summer and then he would put his foot down sure enough.

From the lawn the children's voices drifted up to him. He went to the window and leant on the frame.

Anna sang:
"I think that I shall never see,
A dam more truly pleasing me
But oh the neighbours do beseech,
Because the blasted dam is breached"
"The blasted dam is beached," Liadan shrieked.

Red in the face from running about Liadan came to sit on the front-door steps.

Maurice laughed quietly; Anna was in a teasing mood. Oh he loved it. "That is the thing," he thought. Anna would know how to treat Tom.

Away in the distance Felicity attacked the bamboo where it had escaped into her well-kept lawn. She mowed the lawn; she dug her flowerbeds. He loved her completely even though sometimes he thought a little sheepishly that he would have been happier with a woman who needed him more. He knew how she spent her days and yet there were things that he did not understand, and the reason for her obvious satisfaction remained a mystery. To him large parts of her day seemed to be taken up with turning the place upside down. The house and garden evolved, growing through gradual updates, according to Felicity, but to him changing so fast he wondered sometimes which room he was in. Why could a room not be completed? Then he would be able to find things. He laughed and refilled his glass.

He returned to the window. An evening breeze sent the heavy hall door banging. Anna waved to him. Something about her made him want to look at her a second time, but she had disappeared down the rhododendron path. What, he wondered, had made him start? A physical difference, a sort of urgency? He looked around, craning his neck in order to have a full view of the lawn. Paddy had vanished and Liadan sat on the grass; she threw gravel at the water fountain. Moments later he heard Felicity speak crossly to her. His thoughts slipped back to Anna. He remembered Catherine, his dead wife, had had a way of looking that Anna often had. On their wedding day, as his young bride, she had put herself in his hands. He had not earned either her love or her trust, but she had been young and shy, looking to him for companionship and support. Felicity was different. She had lived her life alone, she had told him, and had learned to be strong. Her need had diminished with age, while his had grown. He was old and soft; he acknowledged it. This was not a fault, it was nature. He wanted Felicity and his daughters to cling to him, to tell him that they loved him and bear witness to and corroborate the sustenance that he gave them, but Felicity had no need and perhaps Anna was growing away from him.

Anna flounced back again into Maurice's view. Had they had a tiff? he wondered.

"Anna," he shouted from the window. "Come in and keep me company,"

Moments later she stood at the dining-room door. Was there a slightly disappointed look in her eyes? Maurice's face smiled, while his heart softened.

"Has Paddy gone home?" he asked more for the sake of something to say. Anna nodded her head.

She stuck her finger into the lemon mousse and scooped the lemon cream into her mouth.

"Have a plate," Maurice said, but she shook her head.

"You know the Fitzwilliams are entertaining tonight, most of the neighbourhood in fact." He noticed as he spoke how alert and attentive to his words she became, almost aggressively so. A smile broke out; her usual vitality had come back.

"Oh that would explain it," she spoke quickly.

"Yes," he said. "I suppose they expected Paddy to go home after work. I don't know what he was doing back here?" His eyes twinkled.

"How did you know about the party?" she asked idly, her eyelids lowered, her fingers intent on polishing her sandal strap.

Maurice took little trouble about any sensitivities she might have. He did not want to go back over the afternoon. He would be brief.

"Tom was at the lake; he said they were entertaining tonight, and why he thought we'd be interested I don't know."

"Oh Daddy we're not," she laughed "We're going to the mountains tomorrow...come with us please?"

"Not tomorrow darling," he smiled at her "and Paddy can't," Maurice warned.

"No!" Anna said, "Doesn't matter."

CHAPTER 9

*S*ome days later Tom came again to the lake. We had a lot *of trouble with leaks and the surging muddy water had broken his pump, or so he said. But the dam had been fixed days before he appeared.*

***

It was the last day they would spend on the lake. The bank looked sturdy and the water played on the pebbled shore fresh and inviting. This last day was a day of hazy, listless, heavy air. Maurice and Paddy had worked by the shelter resetting a broken step before moving on that afternoon to work on the jetty. Thunderstorms were in the air, hovering and suspended, threatening and retreating, while the two continued to work through into the evening. Both watched with gladness the sun moving behind the Cedar trees, but neither remarked on it; they were as silent as the air over the lake. Puffs of air-born dandelion seed slowly floated down into the water. Newly fallen reeds dipped their heads near the edge. Some sturdier stems stood straight, buoyed up by the rising water, while the rotten reeds of a previous season lay hay-dry in the sunshine not far from the jetty. A varied assortment of flies landed and took off. The donkey appeared and stood expectantly by the boathouse. His neck free of his usual harness, he rubbed it up and down on the boathouse door before positioning himself for a full body rub, making the boathouse creak. He looked about furtively as though readying himself for the usual invasion of children and when none came he leant into the water to drink.

Like the donkey Paddy was looking around uneasily. He seemed subdued and spoke only in answer to direct questions. To Maurice he seemed sulky, as Liadan might have been. But

Maurice was not bothered about Paddy's heaviness of heart nor could he see that he was smouldering with hate. Each shovel reminded Paddy of his father's taunts.

***

"If that moron wanted to mend his bank quickly he would use a mechanical digger not a child." Tom's voice, though strangely emotional, went unnoticed by Paddy; only the words cut deep.

"He is using a digger," Paddy retorted. "He still needs help to drive the digger and spread the stones. If I am there I can control the amount of water let out. I thought that's what you wanted?"

"Oh rubbish, Patrick!" A sneer appeared on Tom's upper lip. And not for the first time Patrick was filled with hatred for his father.

Paddy knew his father liked to appear a riddle to him; sometimes he accused Paddy of too much fraternisation with the Agans, only to follow with some obscene remarks aimed at encouraging him to seek greater intimacy with Anna – "Oh I know what you want," Tom would say his face twisted lecherously, "but can you make it happen, my big fellow?"

Paddy was a quiet boy who enjoyed filling the summer days with practical and purposeful activity. He liked his work at Tuskar House for many reasons: he loved to be near Anna and it was a relief to be away from the conflictual atmosphere of his own home. He appreciated the obvious family affection that existed between Maurice and his daughters. Maurice was not an easy person but he treated Paddy well and Paddy had grown fond of him.

When Tom and Jane told Paddy that he had to leave Tuskar, Paddy would have ignored his father, it would have been a pleasure, he had thought, but not his mother. She was angry and noisy, so unlike anything he had ever seen before. In the end she was the one who insisted the most. He knew that what his mother hinted at could not be true. His father, he felt, was only the debris of a person, but his mother... it destroyed him to think of her. Now unexpectedly the filth of that man had rubbed off on her; why did she take his side? Why did she love him the way she did? Paddy could not accept or understand. It would turn him against her in the end. Yet he loved his mother; she twisted his insides, but he loved her. That man tricked her all the time. Her arm crept around Tom as they both insisted. He felt abandoned by her; he would never forgive her. All his life she had stood up for him, but not this time it seemed. Leave today, they told him. He had only three weeks to go and they wanted to destroy the little time he had left, these few weeks of happiness.

During his time at Tuskar, Paddy would have said that he felt happy, contented too, if that had been the sort of word he would have used. Sometimes when he worked a long day he would feel a surge of euphoria, or something akin to that, and when Anna came down to the lake they would walk away from Maurice to swim. Anna would swim close to him making his heart pound and his chest tight so that his breath came quickly. She would shout and splash and talk ten to the dozen. Sometimes in mid sentence she would drive deep into the water with a flash of her toes smacking the surface, only to reappear just by his ear a moment later speaking about something else, as if she had continued to talk under water. Nothing she did surprised him. The joy of her nearness freed him and gave him flair and vigour. It was as though the environment was filled with the force of mutual understanding and the usual changing surface of human interaction had been smoothed: they knew what to expect from each other and when to expect it; it was such easy sailing that it should have continued for ever.

Liadan would run along the shore of the lake shouting to them.

"Gad's sister is here," she would say, announcing Wendy's arrival and giggling, or "Joe's come."

Within seconds their wonder world would disappear: they would have to leave the light behind. For Paddy the memory helped to relieve the hurt of having to share her; a hurt that cut him as sharply as the cut of pampas grass. They gathered together, Wendy, Joe and Liadan, sometimes others, crowding around complaining of the cold, until one by one they ventured in. Liadan would appear swimming around tall reeds. She reminded him of a small fluffy duckling. She bobbed more than the others as she swam. Paddy loved her. She was mischievous. Wendy said she was a brat; she did not like Liadan always being part of their grown-up group. Paddy understood Anna better than Wendy. It was not in her nature to reject. Wendy might try to explain to Anna - younger sisters were nuisances. But Anna's generosity, which enveloped everyone and everything, would never allow her to say no to Liadan. That was how she was made. No other girl that he knew would be willing to put the happiness of others before her own. She had helped Paddy to regain some belief in himself. She had helped him to bear the bitter harm Tom had carelessly done him.

"Anna, do something...that sister of yours!" Wendy would complain and Anna would catch Liadan and swing her about. She would place Liadan on Paddy's shoulders and order him to swim to the bottom of the lake and stay there.

"Let's play mermaids," Liadan would beg, unmoved by Wendy, and immediately Anna would break bulrushes and twist the dark brown flowers into garlands for her.

***

Thinking all day of these things did not make Paddy feel better. Anna had gone to Dublin and he desperately wanted to see her. He just had to talk to her, to tell her they were making him leave.

Now he saw his father coming on the scene; his temple throbbed unbearably in anticipation. Tom strode towards them, shouting scornful taunts.

***

Tom shouted and I tried to calm him down. He pointed his rifle at me, while continuing to abuse me, and I became afraid of what he might do. Paddy moved as fast as he could from the jetty; the sedge grass which was growing thickly in the shallow water slowed him down. We were shouting at each other. I cannot repeat the words he used to describe Felicity: intimate things; these were in order to prove, he said, how well he knew her, but then he started on about Anna and something snapped in me. I snatched the rifle from him and threw it away. Paddy, as he came towards us, caught it. My first full punch aimed at Tom's nose split open his eye as my bare knuckle slid from nose to cheekbone. Mucous and blood gushed out and I got in another punch which dug deep into Tom's solar plexus, winding him. He reeled backwards trying to save himself from further injury, but he had no chance against me. I was fit. I wasn't just a gentleman farmer. Tom's attempts were feeble in comparison. He tried to hit back against the rain of punches. I watched him teeter and settle. He wiped his face with his hand and I said, "Have you had enough then, you ....!"

"You play rough Moorees," he said recovering himself. Next minute Paddy was upon us and he sneered "Here's my little fellow late as usual. Did you know Moorees, he was hoping to have his wicked way with Anna, but he'll fail."

I hit him again very hard, and as he fell backwards Paddy swung the rifle, catching him with one devastating blow.

Tom clutched his chest as he fell, which makes me suspect that neither of us were responsible for his death.

I want to leave you in no doubt that we were not the aggressors. I am sure Tom had slumped forward before Paddy struck him. Poor Paddy thought he had killed his father. I had presumed that Paddy's blow had been meant for me. It was only later, when Jane told me that Tom and Paddy had never got on, that I understood the blow had hit the mark. Tom had ordered Paddy to give up his work here and Paddy had lost control. He could not bear to hear the ugly way that he spoke of Anna, and having to leave her was breaking his heart.

***

Maurice's adrenaline levels were screeching out for more. He stood over Tom's hated and diminished form, twisted, but still. Every trace of the arrogant man had gone, only the poor feeble empty skin seemed to remain. Maurice bore witness but he felt no pity; he was unmoved.

***

Remember before you blame me too much that Tom had a rifle until I disarmed him. I am sure he died from a heart attack. I buried him in the shelter.

***

Liadan cried; large tears trickled down her nose. She reread her father's words. She had known it all, she told herself: there was no need to be upset, but still she cried and cried until she fell asleep.

Later she awoke to moonlight shining through her sash window. She stood a while gazing into the half-lit sky. The birds had gone to bed and a night-time hush had fallen; floating scent from the honeysuckle drifted in through the open window. It was the sort of bright night, warm, sweet-smelling and a little damp that Anna had loved. She would have wandered through the meadows in the newly fallen dew. Liadan stretched out her arm as if to greet her. At quiet times she thought of Anna: the twilight times before sleep or after rising. "What had made Anna so different?" she often wondered. Anna had been fearless and true and she had also been strong and gentle and it was because these qualities lit up her face, conditioned her movements and informed her actions that people stopped to watch her pass, were drawn to her and competed for her company. Liadan could not imagine walking alone through the night and even less could she imagine loving someone so intensely as to lose the desire to live because they had gone away.

Thinking back to her father's letter Liadan realised that, after she had understood that Tom had died on the shore, she had always thought the body was in the lake. Where else could he have been buried? She had ignored "Maurice's stories" and as she had got older the only rational explanation seemed to be - Tom had been dumped in the lake.

***

My Darling, it is quite safe to swim in the lake, the lake water is as pure as it has always been. When I saw you yesterday you were so angry. You told me to write everything down. After which you went to the lake. I wondered were you swimming in that awful water. It's pure but it holds so much horror: for your sake I have always wanted to come to terms with what happened to Anna and I have never wanted you to live your life in her shadow. Even though I suspected you swam there, I didn't ever want to know for sure, because I wanted to avoid the need to ask you not to. Do you understand Lia? Trying to let you have your head has not always been easy but Felicity, I and dear Lucy wanted you to be able to accept Anna's death and see it as tragic but natural.

***

Poor Daddy! Liadan thought. He could not have known that she had not swum south of the jetty for years? She felt weary. Was she now to live continuously with these feelings of regret and remorse? To remember her rages against Maurice upset her. After all nothing had been his fault. He could have been killed! Why had he so insisted on waiting to tell her what she should have been told years ago?

With Felicity out for the evening and Wendy and Lucy gone home, for the first time in months Liadan was alone. Lucy had left a message on the kitchen table. "Ronan rang!" nothing else. She thought of Ronan and a smile spread over her face, fading again as she remembered the tiresome Ronan of their childhood. She wondered now what he would think if he found out that Tom's body was buried in the shelter. It was the last place anyone would think of looking; no one had gone there again after Anna died.

She took the food that Lucy had left her and went back to her room, this time to finish reading her father's letter no matter how much it hurt.

***

Anna's death changed everything. After it forgiving that family became impossible and that is why you will not find any words of regret for Tom. The only regret is that you were a witness. You came running towards us, your bucket swinging wildly, splashing out water and eels. The sight of us both fighting horrified you. Your little face still haunts me. As you ran down the grassy bank you tripped, tumbling over and over, somehow hitting your forehead on the rough ground. It's difficult to know exactly what happened: you were some distance from us.

***

"You... come back." Maurice bellowed. Again he shouted at Paddy. Automatically Paddy had dropped the rifle on the shore. He seemed to be running away, but in fact he had run to Liadan's side. Liadan lay like a discarded doll, a trickle of blood on her forehead. With a face as pallid as a ghost Paddy knelt down. His hands shook. Maurice arrived seconds later.

"You're all right." Maurice whispered. He tenderly lifted her head onto his lap; the cut ran across her forehead an inch below her hairline.

"What happened Lia?"

Liadan opened her wet eyes; she blinked a bit.

"Did you fall over?" Maurice asked. He looked around - stones and twigs, brambles and an uneven terrain; any of these could have caused her to fall over, grazing her head on a stone as she fell. He had seen her running towards them; somehow he had blanked out her presence. Her bucket lay empty by her feet. Now in playback time he could hear her voice calling him and it filled him with grief.

"It's OK, it's OK!" he hushed the voices in his head. "You must have tripped."

"Someone pushed me." Liadan decided. "And then I fell over." She enjoyed the attention. She smiled up at the two of them. They both smiled back at her.

Then she remembered, "Why were you shouting Daddy?"

She seemed alert, but he had to question her anyway.

"What's your name?"

"That's silly," she replied, "You're my Daddy." Her voice took on a scornful edge. And then she said, "Anna!" and laughed.

"Are you?" he laughed too.

"But she's not Anna." Paddy sounded hysterical.

"Good God Paddy, she's teasing. Ask a silly question...! You're fine, my Lia." He patted her on the cheek "Take her to the house Paddy; be quick! Tell them I'm coming but don't say a word about what's happened…Do you understand?"

The incongruity of his request only came to him later and by then Paddy had already gone.

"You're shouting again Daddy, you're making my head hurt." Concern crept into the child's voice.

Maurice struggled; he must not lose control. He had to make decisions and the best way to gain control would be to gain time.

He leant forward. Under no circumstances must Liadan know what had happened.

"Lia, I'm just going to have a little word with Paddy. It's a secret," he said, "about a big present I'm going to buy for a very good, brave girl." He leant back, grabbing Paddy roughly and whispered in his ear.

"Don't let her see anything…you know! Place your hand above her face when you lift her up. Tell no one…do what needs doing and nothing more." He spoke in rushed, staccato sentences, and then no longer whispering, "Carry her up to the house and come back here. Stay calm! Liadan is all right: she's just banged her head. I'll see to things here." He went on giving instructions; needing to.

Paddy struggled into a standing position and Maurice kept himself between Liadan and the body. She tried to look past him, somehow sensing that they did not want her to.

"Don't struggle, Pussy Cat, Paddy will drop you." He leaned over and kissed her again.

Above the lake the eerie air gathered into a cloud which moved in over the silent body as though in collusion with the scene. The moment seemed to have lost all movement and the world to have changed from one still to another, the intervening events being extinguished in denial.

***

I had you taken to the house. Having at first panicked completely I decided to hide Tom's body. I would then, I thought, go to see Jane. I can't explain why I did what I did. The urgency to hide the body from you and everyone else was so strong.

***

Paddy's young body shook as he turned and saw his father's form. He wondered if time was moving on or was he walking towards the house in a slowly repeated loop. He seemed to make little progress and then to find himself down by the lake shore starting the climb again. He tried hard to push ahead, even to walk faster to escape with Liadan from the pull of Tom's body. He struggled to quicken his steps, to run, but his speed did not increase. He could hear Maurice shouting at him and he knew he could not be dreaming.

"Don't jig her about, walk calmly!"

Liadan whimpered a bit in agreement.

Again he heard Maurice call, "I'll be there in a minute. Felicity will look after you, Lia. Come back straight away, Paddy!" Maurice's voice sounded high-pitched to Paddy's sensitive ears and, even stranger, Paddy felt that he could have heard a leaf falling off a tree, so painfully acute his hearing seemed to have become.

A burst of summer wind caught Liadan's hair, blowing it into Paddy's face so that he could hardly see the ground. It hid the tears that fell, blurring his vision but Liadan felt them fall. He had no voice to console Liadan, not that she needed his comfort. It would have upset him had he known how much she was enjoying the drama: like the pictures of dead heroes, she allowed her limbs to flop. For once he would not have forgiven her her childlike ways. He struggled up past the banks of crocosmia. The house looked as it always looked in the summer evening light - tall, solid and resistant to change like an old wellingtonia. The sun had broken through again and washed it in a terracotta glow. Felicity's walls of water, although switched off, left the stainless-steel frames holding mirror images of the house glinting with residual drops. Paddy would always remember walking up the steps, as though in a dream, with the last of the light reflecting off Maurice's car glinting in through the fanlight of the hall door. Ahead of him, as he entered the house, the stairway rose up to high windows that seemed to reach up to the rooftop, sending down to him a solid corridor of light to summon him forward.

"Her head seems to be more bruised than cut," Felicity remarked. "How do you feel? I think you should rest. Paddy will tell you a story. Won't *you* Paddy?"

"I don't want to go to bed," Liadan said, she yawned. "It's only six o'clock. He'll think I'm a baby," she whispered to Felicity.

Paddy stood in the doorway. He longed to stay with Liadan. How he dreaded the walk back to the lake and to all that awaited him there. "Was this a dream?" he asked himself. What had he done? He had to go. He had never in his life experienced such a feeling of doom. His head spun; his mouth was dry; he felt hollow with fear. How could he hold it together? Where would he get the strength to do what he knew would be Maurice's angry bidding? When, if ever, would this Sword of Damocles be lifted?

All the time Felicity arranged Liadan's farmyard animals on her round table.

"We haven't seen much of your parents lately, Paddy," she said.

All the nerves in his body screeched. He wanted to put his hand over her mouth to silence her. He looked at Liadan in fright. Would she remember something? Would she ask some question that now he could not answer calmly? He leant his back against the doorpost needing a crutch, needing to draw some strength from the old oak. Icy sweat trickled down his back and his hands were clammy.

"I'll have to go now," he said in a thin voice. "I have to go," he tried again.

Startled, Felicity cocked her head to one side and peered bird-like at him, she laughed and said:

"*You go* if you have to." She smiled down at Liadan. "He has to *go*, darling!"

Liadan had closed her eyes; the words seemed to bring her back from sleep; a little smile played around her mouth and then she turned to snuggle beneath the covers.

"Tell Maurice everything is all right. I don't think I need call the doctor. Oh and Paddy... remind him that we're going out to-night." She checked her watch. "If he wants to eat he will have to hurry." Paddy crept from the room, too afraid to stay. As he made his way down the corridor he heard Felicity ask herself:

"What's the matter with him?"

CHAPTER 10

Maurice dragged Tom's body close to the edge of the water. His half-hearted resuscitation attempt had made him gag. Now the taste of Tom would stay with him until the time of his own death, a taste of acetone and a sweet smell in his nostrils. He lowered Tom down and gazed at his face. The fight had left some general swelling and the butt of the rifle had crushed his eye. Matted wet hair, blood and skin fragments trickled down past his cheekbone on to his bluish neck. He started to wash the blood away dabbing Tom's face tenderly, and then he stuck his own head into the shallow water, keeping his mouth open wide. He moved his head from side to side like a flamingo sift-feeding, taking in water, mud and gravel, but the taste remained.

How would he face what was ahead of him? Maurice, despite his rumbustious and unruly nature, was not a violent man. No analysis of the actions and reasoning of his life up to the moment in which he found himself could have arrived at the conclusion that he would one day be frantically trying to hide the dead body of his neighbour.

On he dragged Tom towards the underground shelter. There was a suitable place to lay the body down, he remembered, just below a ledge where the ground was stony and firm. When he reached the ledge he sat down just above the dead man to wait for Paddy. Until Paddy came back, he would not do another thing.

Instinct took over and a strong sense of self-preservation: time would not be his only enemy; panic would be fatal. He had to get rid of the evidence; this was the most important thing. All the time he continued to try to justify what had occurred. His head buzzed with warnings and his overwhelming desire was to hide what he could, as quickly as he could; to hide what had happened; to wipe everything out. The sight of Tom's battered face was the brutal evidence of his unmistakable guilt. His eyes were drawn to it as though it were a work of art. If he could get the body to the shelter, no one would see it there. It was not going to be an easy feat even for a couple of strong men, but he could not achieve it alone. Then, how would he explain what had happened to the police - to Jane? When Paddy came back they would speak to Jane together. She would have to be told that Tom had attacked him first. In reality he was the injured party. Felicity had nothing to do with any of this, no matter what they thought. Yet for a moment he wanted to curse Felicity, and then he remembered he had spoken of his jealousies to her and she had come to him that night.

Maurice put his head in his hands. In the whole of his life he had never felt like this: a burning, bursting feeling inside his veins; he wanted to roar; he wished he could hit out at something.... Paddy had struck the most vicious blow, it had not been him; he would not let Jane forget that.

He stood up, "What am I doing, I should ring the police straight away," he said aloud. He did not move; his feelings of guilt were too acute, too intense. "It's just too late, oh God... too late." He sat down again. He had no intention of running to the police, he told himself. The battered body of Tom made that impossible; the evening light lit the damage clearly. His fingerprints were on the rifle. There was not a person in the district who had not heard him fulminating about how he wanted to kill the man.

He had to speak to Jane soon. Where was Paddy? Why did the boy not come back? Maurice stood up and paced and fumed aloud. "Where's that stupid boy? I told *them* he was useless...that fool...he'll have us all in jail. That bastard family." He roared.

He broke into a run over the dry expanded shore, around the shelter to reach the boathouse. Within minutes the boat was afloat with him sitting in it, powering back his oars, slicing and ladling water behind him to sweep him back towards the lifeless form. From the lake the body looked like a beached seal.

The sight spurred him. The urgency he felt to hide the corpse had taken him over. Tampering by some wild animal would be unthinkable, but it was hardly likely where the largest carnivore would far prefer a fat chicken stolen from the hen run. No! The overriding need was to hide his guilt away.

It was an impossible task for one person: no matter what he did he could not get the body into the boat. As soon as he lifted one limb, the other became lodged underneath, making the boat slide further out into the water. Maurice hauled and hauled and the weight of Tom made the boat buck away. His energy and strength were used up; he felt weak with the effort; he was gasping for air. Eventually almost incapacitated with the rage of failure he pulled the boat right out of the water, scraping its bottom viciously on the rough stones. Tom lay like a discarded doll on the shore, with one leg bent so that the knee stood up in a relaxed attitude. Maurice collapsed beside the body, overcome by an almost demented frenzy.

Still that boy had not come back!

The water lapped gently. A flock of green finches swept down to the water's edge to drink, and then as quickly were gone. The cloudless sky turned pink and cream as the sun fell below the dark-green trees. Pigeons came in to roost. Their wings flapped audibly; their greetings reminiscent of evening time.

For a moment Maurice considered using the digger to bury Tom but he knew, being so close to the house, the noise would attract attention. Instead he anchored down the boat by adjusting the arm of the digger. He reached under Tom's shoulders, clasping him tightly, and struggling hauled him upwards. The weight made his hands slip but he grabbed anew, binding the man's shirt around his wrists to gain extra purchase. By the time he had the torso in the boat the shirt had been stripped away and Tom lay, half naked and mud-spattered. To Maurice's amazement his chest seemed unharmed: there was no cavern below the sternum and he looked - almost life-like. But Maurice had no time to consider any of this; he had to hurry. He removed two seating planks and following a determined push the body slid on to the bottom of the boat.

Now with the body stowed, he had time to think. In the end he wouldn't need Paddy's assistance. Managing alone allowed him all the control and he needed that. He could cope with everything; time was running out but he was in charge.

**

Anna stood in the hallway, a towel slung over her shoulder. She spoke to Lucy in a hushed voice, her head bent forward. Her hair was tied in a knot on the top of her head. She had a child-like solemnity as she spoke and, although Maurice did not catch the words, he caught the anxiety in the air and he rushed to dispel it. Lucy leant on the banisters with purpose. She wanted to know what had happened to her baby. Maurice would have to answer her questions before any other; he could tell by the solid way she stood. Lucy had been with them for too long; she had seen too much and her affection for the family was so great that her insistence on being kept informed, on knowing where everybody stood and how things really were, could not be considered in any way an impertinence. Maurice knew how much he owed to Lucy and how surely his life would have been rendered impossible after his wife's death without her.

"The poor love...I'd best see her," she muttered. Liadan would need her.

But Maurice wanted to calm her inquisitiveness and get her back to the kitchen.

"Oh it's nothing; she's fine. She fell by the lake. Sorry about the mud." All contrition, he looked down at his boots. He grasped her shoulders in a friendly hug and said in a little-boy voice.

"What's for dinner Fast and Loosey," and he licked his lips.

"Get off with you," she said, and laughed obediently for him. "Nothing is the answer. Ugh, what a mess!" She turned on her heel and, being reassured, did not insist. There was nothing strange, no story, and as she said to the girls when questioned, nothing had happened that night.

How much Felicity noticed of his disarray remained unclear to Maurice, but had she known, he was sure that she would have been definite in her response. She would never have left him, or would she? They exchanged their usual few words on the landing. He did not speak of Liadan - there was no need to worry about her just now; he had other matters on his mind. He felt that he had to be careful with Felicity, but luckily she also had other things on her mind.

"Where's Paddy?" he asked.

"He's gone home. It's *quite late* you know." She put on her this-isn't-good-enough voice and said "You'll need to hurry or we'll *be* late. Oh dear *the very state* of you."

"Late, what do you mean, late?" His heart sank.

"The opera silly; don't you remember? Really you are *too much.*"

"What!" Maurice's heart pumped faster.

"I *told* Paddy to tell you to hurry. It's Cinderella- *Rossini*; you said you loved it."

"Can't you get someone else to go?" he implored her. "I wouldn't be ready in time. Anna can go."

"Anna and Wendy are going." There was a long silence and then she shook her head. "*Never mind,* I'll ask Freda..." She threw the words over her shoulder ...already on her way to call Freda.

He made for the stairs but she came back after him.

"*Where* do you think *you're* going now? Liadan shouldn't be left alone...and..."

"Of course," he tried to smile, relax his shoulders, "I need to go back to the lake to put the tools away... and the boat. I have one or two little things to do in the yard. Lucy and I will see to Liadan," he said, and then, "Enjoy your evening." His voice quaked with stress.

He continued on and she kept with him, a speculative smile on her face.

"Wait a minute." She eyed him from one eye, like a bird.

Maurice held his breath, but then she seemed to change tack and asked in almost a normal voice, "A *small* request, darling

...and considering the *hot water* you're in..." her eyes were watching him closely he felt, but she leant over and kissed his lips. "Take Lucy home...if she's going to baby-sit she needs to get home to be back in time. I promised I'd take her myself and I..."

Maurice started to protest, "Can't someone else...Anna ...?" He asked desperately. He had so much to do.

"Poor Anna ...Mm...*you're in a hurry*...really Maurice."

"OK, OK," he came in quickly.

"Lucy needs to put *something* in the oven for Charley ...I'm sure *she won't be long*...we might be back a bit late...the crowd from Templeslaney will be there and we thought we'd have a late supper..." She stopped and looked puzzled, "Funny thing, Paddy didn't seem to know about his parents going to the opera, as bad as you...Mmm"

Maurice felt the colour leave his face; he knew he had to smile.

"I'll take Lucy, you go," he said quickly, "Go on, have a good time!" He tried to walk down the stairs in a carefree manner. He straightened his back and hummed but when he got to the kitchen he let rip: "Lucy," he roared, "into the car!" and he marched down the hall with Lucy trotting behind him. Down the avenue he raced.

"What's up with you? You're drivin' like a looney." Lucy huffed, "I'm gettin' out and walkin' if you don't behave," she warned.

"I'm in a hurry Lucy. It's the dam... I need to get back or all the work we've done today will be wasted, so please, nice Lucy, do hurry feeding that old fellow of yours."

***

He slipped from the house and immediately broke into a run. The pathway was clear and dry. He was hoping anxiously to catch up with Paddy, but by the time he reached the lake Paddy was nowhere to be seen. The boat stood alone, shielded from exposure by the grassy shelf. Suddenly a picture of Paddy with the rifle flashed into his mind and he raced about looking for it. God! Where had Paddy thrown it or had he picked it up? He could not remember; there were so many tapes playing in his head at different speeds that it was like a market place on fair day, but nowhere could he find an image involving the rifle. "Before it gets dark," he kept thinking, "I must find it."

***

It's important to know that the decisions we made that evening were all decided on by the three of us: Jane Fitzwilliam, Paddy and myself. I couldn't have done anything without their full support and assistance.

Why did we behave as we did? My answer would have to be: "It was safer than going to court and possibly to jail". We were innocent; yet we all acted in a guilty manner. I felt under terrible pressure to act. Jane was very insistent, though later she blamed me for what happened.

***

Following the path that he considered Paddy must have taken, Maurice left his own land and crossed the river on to *Pastures New*, the Fitzwilliams' property. Maurice had never been able to enter their land without some mocking comment or thought regarding the name they had chosen, but on that night the name never even occurred to him. A hill shielded the properties from each other and the river Galley ran as a boundary between the lands. *Tuskar Rock House* was the area's largest house and proud of its position. *Pastures New*, though once a humble abode had been greatly embellished and had taken on quite a new entrepreneurial air. Its size had doubled and the careful planting of trees, bushes and fast-growing creepers hid all that was less noble and enhanced all that was fine. The fineness and the enhancement had a skin-deep quality, a little like that of its owners. It was at the same time affluent and aspiring, but it was difficult to know to what. Maurice had often thought that there was an awful lot of it and perhaps a little less would have been more convincing.

He crossed the lawn, coming up out of a sunken area, and as he appeared at the top of the rise the setting sun threw a gigantic shadow of him upon the house "like a premonition," he thought, "that had come too late."

Jane and Paddy sat in a little room near the rear of the house which was lined with shelves of red and blue ledgers, with binders and folders strewn on the floor. Two large desks faced each other by a casement window that looked out on to a small courtyard, which in turn looked on to a walled kitchen garden. A black spaniel dog stood by the window, rubber ball in mouth, tail ready to wag, but somewhat distrustful of Maurice's arrival.

The "his" and "her" desk arrangement had allowed Jane and Tom to be close to one another while working and now Tom's place was taken by a very tense Paddy. Jane held Paddy's hand while they consoled each other. The picture of the two of them made Maurice hesitate and he remained standing in the doorway. As he expected Jane gasped at his sudden appearance, her hand clasping her mouth. Maybe she thought the footsteps might have been someone else. When she had regained her composure, she became decisive; it was not what he had expected.

There were plates and wine glasses close by, reminding Maurice that he had not eaten; his stomach rumbled loudly and expressively, and the banality made him smile wryly. He had come prepared for an almighty struggle but instead Jane invited him to eat and she put a glass of brandy in front of him.

"We have a lot to decide," he said almost as soon as Maurice sat down. "We must try to do the best thing for Paddy," she continued and here her voice had a steely quality. "Nothing will bring Tom back...my son is not going to be punished because of you and Tom. Never...I won't allow it...I warn you."

"I don't..." Maurice started.

"Your family owes mine..."

"...understand," Maurice ended.

"Paddy is ready to go."

"You want Paddy to leave?" Maurice's vocal cords became stretched with anxiety - had he missed something? If Paddy disappeared, where would that leave him? All the while his brain, which had been functioning like a low, continuous, vibrating sound, planning, arguing, answering hypothetical questions, closed down and all he could feel was a solid condition developing just above his eyes. She had stumped him.

"What are you going to do about Tom?" she asked as if enquiring about a dog.

"He's in the boat." Paddy said.

"You can't just throw him into the lake." There was no emotion in her voice but the sound of a tear drop was heard a moment before she flicked through the papers on her desk.

"So they had seen him," Maurice noted.

"We've had more time than you... we both agree. Paddy must leave, I'll follow later."

Maurice took another drink: the fog in his mind had to lift. Obviously Paddy thought himself more to blame for Tom's death than Maurice had been; why else would he run away? "Yes!" he thought, Paddy wanted to run away because he felt guilt; he knew he had hit his father hard...maybe even meant to. He could have killed him! The seizure that Tom had had might not have been enough. He felt relief: if Paddy had thought differently of Tom's death, things would have looked very bad for Maurice. He had fought Tom fair and square, but who would care, if the son spoke out against him?

"You must go with Paddy on the early morning sailing tomorrow. You will need to drive with Paddy because he must get across England as quickly as possible. I have already made provisional bookings; come back as soon as you are able. Paddy will go on to France and then in a few days' time fly to Kenya. I have family living in Nyarururu. We will all have to be vigilant. If asked, Paddy will say he does not know where his father went and I will say the same. People know his reputation... oh yes, I know." She nodded and her voice shattered. "Tomorrow I will drive to Dublin and dump his car. I will burn his passport and clothing. You can rely on me to do everything to protect Paddy. You will pretend to know nothing. I will be the one to lie and lie and lie, if needs be." Her voice droned on and made his eardrums vibrate.

"Wait a minute…let me think here…I don't want to be rushed…it's all very well but there are so many things that need attending to."

"Fine."

"I couldn't find the rifle, that's just one thing."

"What? No! I dropped it," Paddy said, his voice shaking with fear. "I know I did."

Jane hugged him. They could comfort each other; Maurice felt alone.

He drank and ate and tried to think. He drank again. He realised all that he would still have to go through: he would have to bury Tom; he would have to search for that rifle. There would be no one to comfort him. He thought of Liadan, his innocent little girl frightened, staggering towards him. When she woke up what would she remember? He spoke aloud without thinking.

"You should be very grateful that I am agreeing to any of this."

Jane shot to her feet – she was small, but she terrified him, snarling with fury, her black clothes and heavily-lined eyes against her ivory skin, made her look like a witch. Her blueberry-coloured lips ugly in their clown-like grimace.

"How dare you, you fool! How dare you!" She shouted over the desk at him. "Your family is the cause of all of this. Your awful adulterous…"

Paddy grabbed her hand; he pulled her back to her seat. Tears were running down his face, he looked so vulnerable. "No Mummy," he begged, "Please."

"Finish here…" she hugged Paddy to her. "Get to the ferry as soon as you can, we'll be waiting."

Still he couldn't stop the spinning in his head. He wanted to ask her why? Why are you pushing for Paddy's departure? Why don't you grieve for Tom? Why don't you blame me more? I hit him…maybe I killed him, why?

Her voice held no emotion when she spoke of Tom. He rose from his seat.

"Finish your sandwiches! You'll need the energy. You'll have to manage as best you can. I have two hurricane lamps ready for you. You've at least an hour of reasonable light – then a full moon." Her voice faded.

He spoke back in a matter of fact way. "Yes I'll manage. Be ready to leave any time after... you buy the tickets and I'll drive him across for the channel crossing. This has all been a terrible mistake. I wonder are we doing the right thing?" His voice got thin like an old man's.

"There is no going back," she said.

And Maurice remembered the battered face and knew he would not be the one to tell the police what he had done.

CHAPTER 11

*I*f *Tom is found in your lifetime, (the possibility becomes more real everyday because of the bypass) I don't want you thinking that I murdered him. I want you to be in a position to defend our name.*

***

While Maurice rowed the boat to the shelter the light was good. The air was cold over the water but Maurice hardly noticed, although he shivered. The corpse lolled about with the irregular lapping beneath the boat, before settling down motionless once the boat had reached deeper water. He kept his eyes resolutely ahead: being so near, the body spread a blanket of dread which suffocated him. The time passed quickly, yet every second seemed crucial, so many things had to be dealt with; there was no leeway for mistakes; the margins were so tight, like the feeling in his chest. Tom must be buried and everything put away so that Anna and Liadan would find nothing to upset them. He should not be late taking Lucy home; at this hour she would not want to walk. He must be in his bed by the time Felicity and Anna got home from the opera, probably around one in the morning, and then while they were sleeping he would have to leave early for the boat. He shook his head from side to side as though to relieve it. There was no place for agitation or hysteria; his emotions had to be frozen. It was necessary, it must be done; he would do it. And so persuaded, his mind switched to automatic and his limbs obeyed its instructions. He had to hurry if he had any hope of catching that morning sailing.

Some fifteen years previously when the little kitchen and showers were built by the lakeside adjoining the air-raid shelter, they had hauled everything they needed straight from a raft.

The bags of cement, the bricks, even the windows and doors got winched up to the building site. Now Tom's body made the same slow journey. Once ashore Maurice released the winch, dumping Tom onto the bank. He then rowed himself back, keeping close to the shore line to pick up all that had been left behind: the lamps, his spades, shovels and his jacket. It was then he had the good luck to stumble upon the rifle. Lifting it with a certain relief, but also a measure of horror, he laid it on the bottom of the boat. On leaving the area he raked the gravel and scuffled the earth erasing signs of a struggle where he could.

The sky had turned angry as the sun disappeared, then slowly faded and the pale washed-out moon rose above the house, gathering strength as the sky lost its redness. Shadows gained in length, gently covering all solid forms with a dusty cloak, and a delicate quiet filled the air. The sounds of animals faded and the silence of night was only broken by the occasional expression of life. Maurice kept working furiously, hardly aware of the changes.

Placing the body in a half-sitting position in the corridor of the air-raid shelter, he cleared the little room of table and chairs. Soon he had cut a template for a grave in the floor. The soil, damp from the lake, held tight to his shovel and the room's dimensions made it difficult to manoeuvre. The two lamps, strategically placed in order to give him maximum light into and along the passage to the shelter, lit up the claustrophobic chamber, throwing up shadows of him striking the earth with his pickaxe. Maurice did not see the blows shadowed on the wall and was not concerned about being seen or heard, for there would be no one about. The nearest neighbours, the Fitzwilliams, would be packing. Jane would remove Tom's clothes from his wardrobe to make it look as if he had gone away. Later she would grieve for him, Maurice supposed. Then, turning his thoughts to himself: later he would be a happy man; he would not be sorry - but now there was no time to think of later.

A large mound of soil developed by the wall, shovel by painful shovel. It covered most of the little cupboard and almost touched the ceiling on one side and yet he didn't think the hole deep enough: he had seen how graves were dug in graveyards.

"Eleven feet deep for a family." He remembered a gravedigger had told him. "So that Granddad can be put in first, then Grandma nine feet down, Aunt Maud at seven feet with room for a little one on top."

He would manage not more than three feet here, but three feet - would that be enough? Already the hole filled up with water and soon he would need to use the shower-room pump. He dug on and the automatic mode into which he had switched helped him to keep going, not to feel the pain of his muscles, not to feel the despair of his acts.

With no more room around the grave to shovel the earth, he had to stop; a sudden collapse was a possibility: a side might cave in and where would he find the energy to dig it out again. He sobbed at the thought. Massive sodden clay like hands gripped his ankles and his arms were so heavy that to lift another shovel would certainly cost him his life. His breathing filled the chamber and was often accompanied by moans. He glanced down at his hands; they were hard, used to manual labour, but the weals on his palms were bleeding and cracked under the intensity of the digging. Yet he was unaware of their sting; aware only of a throb in his palms and arm muscles. His heart thumped against his ribs. The surge of adrenaline had run out. He felt shocked and the tenseness and tightness of his chest made breathing increasingly difficult.

His mind began to play tricks on him and the story Charley, the yard man, had told to Liadan and himself only a couple of days before flashed into his head. The more he tried to forget it, the more it stood firm in his mind and the more plausible the story seemed to become. Twice he suspected the body moved behind him and he stood, too frightened to breath. Though previously he had tried to resuscitate Tom, now Maurice would have struck him with his spade, such was the overwhelming panic pressing on his brain.

"Stop it," he commanded himself, but to no avail and Charley's voice took over.

* * *

"Not long ago," Charley said.

Even though the impatient Maurice had wanted to shut the old fool up, he had gone on.

"Tell me," Liadan insisted.

They stood in the yard just under the bell in the old archway where the house martins nested, zooming in and out on extended wings, chirping and tweeting, dipping and alighting and filling the air with movement. The heavy rain had stopped and a drizzle dripped gently from the gutters. Beads of bright bubbles of water ran along the telephone wire. Charley's collie rushed backwards and forwards as if he knew the story was a good one.

"Rich old Mrs. Blake," Charley looked grave, "who lived on Lady's Island married a young fellah." Knowing his audience he rushed quickly into the story. "Shortly after the wedding she got sick and died, but woke up when her coffin hit the graveyard gatepost."

"Very good." Maurice snapped.

"Wait a bit." Charley blew his nose in a deliberate way. "After a further six years she died again, only this time the young scoundrel had the graveyard gatepost widened before he would allow the funeral to take place."

Maurice laughed and Liadan let out a long gasp.

"At the graveside, the fellah in an agony to get the diamond ring that had remained on her finger, insisted the coffin be opened, in order he said, to look at her dear face. But as he lent down to kiss her he moved to pull the ring from her finger and … she woke up." Charley made his voice go deep and loud so that Liadan jumped.

"Death's a tricky fellah." Charley took his cap off and patted his dog with it, and the animal whirled around and around.

Liadan thought: "Can you really wake up when you're dead?" she asked.

"Course not." Maurice said. Her little hand slipped into his.

"They do." Charley insisted.

"He's a silly old fool." Maurice said turning his back on Charley and taking Liadan back to the kitchen.

***

People were full of stories about the sudden awakening of corpses. Cold beads of sweat were present on Maurice's scalp and trickled down his neck. That silly tale; he did not believe any of it. He had always been so soundly embedded in reality. He had never felt even the slightest fear with regard to out-of-the-ordinary experiences. His grip on what was around him had always been sufficiently firm that he could allow himself an easy relationship with the extraordinary. The ghost story: he could even have agreed and told a better one himself without any discomfort. Now he was confronted with something so new; he was stuck; he was on quicksand; he had lost control and even though he tried to stop the memory, it exploded in his already overloaded imagination. As he struck the earth he heard someone whisper. He dared not turn around; he was terrified. He had lost all sense of reality. He tried to reassure himself. He imagined Tom smirking at him from behind. He could hear someone breathing and he felt a damp heavy feeling of something moving. His pupils narrowed to pinpricks where they should have dilated in the dark cell-like room. For a moment he became almost blind. Fear had taken over. He swung around and placed his foot against the door frame. He reached into the corridor, scrabbling for Tom's arm. He had to get that body into the grave. He had to stop it frightening him. Summoning all his waning strength he heaved until the body came though like the birth of an elephant, making him lose his footing and fall backwards into the grave he had dug. He lay trapped with the body of Tom on top of him, his arm around his neck as though embracing him. The feel of his naked chest and the smell of his body made his stomach convulse. No one would come to rescue him from this hell. The victim of his act had come back to kill him; this thing was trying to smother him. It whispered his name. It taunted him. He could not get free. He felt a breath pass his cheek like a kiss and the hand stroked his head. The corpse was alive. He screamed in terror, and with the strength of madness he scrambled from the grave. Tearing out of the shelter in this psychotic state, his decision was made as to what he would do.

**

When he shot Tom there had been no outward sign or sound after the first embedding of the bullet, apart from the continuing vibrations of the waves, lapping and lapping, plaguing his ears. Maurice vomited; pieces of sandwich and strings of saliva spewed out. It was useless; he would never be rid of the horror; it would always be with him no matter what he tried to do. He knew even as the first clods of earth hit the body, nothing could rid him of Tom.

He set a small landslide in motion by pushing over the little cupboard. Soon the hollow sound of the earth falling into a less than solid space faded, and earth upon earth became the dominant sound. It had taken him a good two hours. At last the awful imaginings had quietened down; his head felt insubstantial, enlarged, full of air and strained as though full of polystyrene. The feeling of shame that remained was reduced to a low level. Soon even this became submerged in a feeling of dull apathy: he did not care; he felt neither guilt nor fear and nothing would be able to change this. He was a machine and the machine finished the job gradually, leaving him an empty man. A central mound had grown up, shouting out the secret of the body beneath; a mound of large proportions in a tiny room. In his growing indifference he thought of how the body would shrink and after that the floor would settle down.

Light from the lamps flickered, warning him of the time already spent.

Outside again the clean, cool air refreshed him. A certain arrogance surfaced as he stood at the door; he had done it all - alone: the dreadful secret was buried. He leant against the closed door.

The sun was long gone and the apparently translucent moon had risen and darkened. Bats flew past his head, dipping down to the water. He envied them their simple life. Where would he find any compensation for what he had endured? He would rather take on their blinkered existence, never knowing or needing to know. Surely, he told himself, the pain of death would be diluted with a lack of foresight. An owl appeared – silent - light as gossamer, floating in the air. With knowledge of what was to come the unexpectedness of the natural world made his heart ache.

Up he climbed, away from the lake, making a hurried journey around to the back of the house. Tightly clipped laurel bushes and box hedging guarded the many entrances into the outer and inner yards. Maurice entered through the dog kennels, making the working dogs sniff the air and bury their heads into the straw. A small door cut into a larger sliding door allowed him to pass through into a covered passageway that led to the inner courtyard adjoining the house. He clung to the shadow thrown by the building, making a semicircular way to the kitchen window. This high wrought-iron barred window remained open in both summer and winter. A fine mesh kept the larger insects out. Lucy sat reading. Her head and shoulders were crouched over her book and she did not seem to notice him as he looked in at her through the uncurtained window. The room within looked comforting, but watching Lucy made him feel an intruder and when a wet nose pressed into his hand he nearly yelled. Charley's collie was there nuzzling his hand: roaming the yards at night catching rats was a favourite occupation; being with Maurice was another.

The scullery door scraped along the stone floor when Maurice entered but no questioning voice called to him and he wondered what Lucy could be reading to absorb her so. The dog followed him down the stone passageway; only the soft sound of its nails on the stone could be heard and Maurice was glad of the sound. He grabbed two containers of Jeyes Fluid from amongst a variety of disinfectants and poisons and made a hasty retreat. He moved quickly out into the yard, back the way he had come, through the long, moon-lit grass and on down again to the water's edge.

Forcing himself into the dank chamber he battled expectation and dread. He knew why the light flickered but the movement terrified him. Quickly he sprinkled the Jeyes Fluid all about the room, smoothing away all trace of foot prints as he retreated back into the corridor. The smell invaded his nostrils and covered the damp, dank smell of rotting vegetation. He continued to sprinkle the fluid and smooth the ground, until he was satisfied that there would be no smells of flesh to draw vermin and no visible signs to attract inquisitive children. He got back into the boat and rowed again to the jetty.

When securing the boat, Maurice spotted the rifle below the seat planks in the bottom of the boat, but nothing would have made him enter the shelter again. So he took the rifle with him.

For the last time that night he left the lake and slipped in by the kennels and on to the outer yard through the arched iron-studded doorway, where overhead hung the big bell which so often, with its resonating voice, called the men working in the fields and the children playing at a distance back to the house. Without ever leaving the shadows he circled the pools of eerie yellow light that shone from the many street-style lamps about the inner and outer yards. Puddles from the washed churns caught the darkness of the night and mixed it with the reflected light. In this outer yard there were many pitch-black areas in the lee of the buildings and the large gloomy hay barn towered over the cowsheds hiding the moon. Maurice quickly made his way to the cowshed by the bell tower, deserted after the evening milking. During the summer months the cows returned to the fields. He hid the gun, slipping it behind a manger and covering it with a wooden plank which seemed part of the cow stall.

On an old tree trunk outside the cowshed he sat to plan. A hundred irrational thoughts and unconnected memories crowded in on him and Maurice hung his head. How his beautiful daughters would loath him for this evening's work: Anna's heart would be broken if she knew Paddy had gone away; Liadan might remember too much and see a murderer's face instead of his.

Even had there not been these overt aspects of all that had happened, how could the father of these two young girls ever be at peace in their company again? For Maurice a new and frightening life had started this night and though he would continue on now and see it though to the end, he would never recover from the mutilation of the simple and limpid relationship that he had always enjoyed with his children. They were the most important thing in his life.

The dog came to stand beside him placing his muzzle on Maurice's arm, and Maurice in turn placed his bruised hand on the dog's head. The smell of cow's milk and cow's breath gently mingled with the earthy smell of the dog.

After a little time Maurice crept back to the dairy at the back of the scullery block to wash. All sorts of milk churns and measuring jugs hung on the walls, and a concreted floor was contoured and channelled for the easy flow of water towards the channel down the middle. There were ceiling hoses and spray guns overhead. He removed his clothing, dropping them above the channel, and turned on the showers. The cold water flushed down on him and was soon followed with water so hot he had to jump out of its drive. Then the cold water returned fast and furious, bruising his shoulders as large hailstones might have done. All the time the collie kept an eye on him from the doorway. Maurice felt strangely reassured. He washed using harsh detergent that inflamed his skin, brushing his nails again and again until red blood took the place of the black Jeyes Fluid beneath his fingernails. The clothes he placed in a bin bag and, after drying himself, he pulled on a white dairy coat before making his way up to his room to change. He drove Lucy home in almost complete silence; for once she seemed too tired herself to make conversation or ask questions.

The night crept on relentlessly. He wrote a note for Felicity and then lay in bed silent and tense. At four in the morning he rose again and left the house before the sun came up. When

Maurice next rested he was on the boat with Paddy. With Paddy he watched the first faint signs of a new day being born; they stood side by side as the boat set out for Fishguard.

CHAPTER 12

As rays of early morning light shone through the window Liadan awoke; she remembered her nightmare and she started to cry. In the nightmare she had stood by the lake in a stream of cold air that travelled on clouds of mist. Her view of the lake was streaked and narrowed as though she were looking through a Venetian blind. The ribbons of light quivered angrily. She felt uncomfortable to be there, yet could not leave, and a strange mixture of glee and fear possessed her as she watched her father, Paddy and someone else dancing about. She tried to cry out a warning but her lips stuck together and the cry receded down her throat. She felt that she needed to sit down, but she could not satisfy this imperative need because she was already sitting down. The colours in the lake saddened her and the air was filled with a booming voice and then suddenly a loud bang, so loud it almost deafened her. She could not understand what was happening and everything was confused. She drew in an enormous refreshing breath but, like everything else that was happening, it changed and there was no relief and no refreshment and then Anna was sitting by her bed. She knew she had screamed, but after that everything was confusion.

Felicity and Anna were by her bed, calling to her and shaking her.

"I hope this doesn't become a *habit* with her," Felicity said sternly while Liadan sobbed. "*I've been* in and out all night and can't make head nor tail of what *is* wrong."

"What's the matter Lia?" Anna asked. She slipped into the bed. Liadan wanted to look pleased. Usually she would have begged for this treat, but not now, she had to concentrate, she had to speak to them, tell them of the dreadful things that had been happening at the lake.

"Daddy was ... Daddy was... it was awful but I don't know, I can't remember" she screamed.

"Oh *really*!" Felicity said, losing patience.

"Wake up silly!" Anna said.

She knew that she could not make them understand and she fell back exhausted.

Eventually after a long silence Felicity spoke. "Oh well! It's over now," she sighed. She stood by the window her arms folded; she seemed to be talking to herself.

The Rhode Island Red cockerel's strident morning call rang out. The sun had risen, sucking away the mists, leaving another beautiful day ahead. A blue tit appeared at the window fluttering and twitching, clinging on to the Virginia creeper as it spun upside down, quivering its feathers before disappearing into the early morning air.

"Aren't you ever going to bed?" Anna asked at last. "I can look after Lia."

"Anna ..." she spoke to the window not looking back, "something odd has happened; I'm sure of it. At least it's finished now," her voice took on a dreamy quality, "a *dreadful* thing... but it's finished."

Anna slipped from the bed. "What?" She whispered.

Liadan heard and she saw Felicity put her finger to her lips.

"I *don't need* much sleep," Felicity answered and then she laughed in a cold, unamused way. "Maurice is away for a few days. There was an urgent meeting called in Dublin, something to do with some business...I don't know."

When Anna came back to the bed she was pale. Liadan threw her head back on the pillow, longing for the feeling of tension to go. Her hair, catching the light, fanned out like fire fingers framing her face in a bright halo against her pillow.

"You look *so* like the young girl in Cinderella. Isn't she, *Anna*?" Felicity leant over them, "quite a *darling*," her voice had regained its usual neutral aloofness. "I'm off to my room."

"Am I Anna?" Liadan asked when Felicity had left the room. "Am I really?"

Anna kissed her "You are… you really are!"

"Tell me about her," Liadan begged, "pleeese."

"Alright...alright but, Lia, we didn't see all of it as we were so late. Felicity made me sit in the car...she said she wanted to make a further check on you...she took ages...still it was fun."

***

For years Liadan's confused dreams and unexplained memories, like Paddy's discomposure as he had carried her back to the house and the smell of Jeyes fluid on her father's hands when he came to her bedroom to check that she was alright, convinced her something very odd had happened that day. In her mind this was the end of the old times. She felt that nothing would ever be the same again. Perhaps the most salient factor in all the bewildering perplexity of this time was the obvious and concerted attempt by those around her to smooth things over, to dispel and dismiss any idea of an event or happening that might be considered even the smallest bit out of the ordinary. The child was not taken in but could not put any sense on the atmosphere that surrounded her. In general the days got washed one into the other: they were coloured by the change that had taken place. After that night Anna became like someone else; she became fearful, apprehensive and almost paranoid.

***

The Indian summer lingered on into October. At first the warm days concealed and obscured how apathetic Anna had become, sleeping under the cedar trees, sprawling about endlessly in the sun, not eating, never hungry. Liadan complained bitterly and constantly to Maurice that Anna had become boring. Maurice said she was dreaming of Paddy. But her frenetic behaviour of dashing about at night, sometimes mumbling to herself; the wild, unseeing look in her eyes which often changed to one of total despair he could not explain, and it frightened him.

"Didn't you hear her last night?" he had asked Felicity.

"Well the noise *woke me*... I did wonder."

"What is she up to?" He became agitated and loud. "Did you ever behave like this?" But the more he tried to press her, the less time she seemed to have for him.

"*Leave* it!" she advised him when cornered. Much like Anna's pleading of "Leave me!"

He noticed how Felicity rushed to attend to some triviality, or showed impatience as she lingered at a door closing it slowly but firmly, as he tried to get in last words of worry before she had gone. She tapped relentlessly on the steering wheel waiting for him to move away when waylaid in her car. He worried and worried, but she did not want to talk.

"It's so bad for her to be brooding like this," he would try. "When does she eat?"

"Stop *fussing*," Felicity said, "girls *don't* eat...I know ..."

"What...what tell me?" he would ask. "Tell me?" but he was afraid. "Felicity..." he would beg but she had gone. Could she not bear to be with him anymore? He felt adrift, bobbing about in a vast emptiness searching for help. But how could he blame her? Secrets were the core of the problem. She could not possibly know how he felt when he did not tell her, when he gave her no inkling of why he was so disturbed.

He remembered arriving back from the boat having been missing for 48 hours, unwilling to account for himself, still frightened and very depressed. They had met on the stairs. He should have told her then; he had had an opening. She had looked at him hard and said.

"You don't *look* much better," signalling that others might be listening.

"No?"

"I rang Mary Brady this morning to *cancel* dinner tonight; I said you were still unwell."

He hung his head in weariness, "Oh!"

She continued, "It's rearranged for Wednesday fortnight...Is that alright?"

He nodded his acquiescence without really understanding. He stood still, almost too tired to move now that he had stopped climbing the stairs. Where should he go? What should he do?

He found himself unable to make any decision; his mind fighting against even thinking. He had been puzzled but relieved that she did not ask where he had been.

"Did they think it odd?"

"Of course not. I told her you'd picked up the tummy bug that Liadan had last week."

"Will I pop in to see her?" he had wondered aloud.

"Go to bed," she had ordered him. "She's fine."

Everyone knew little girls picked up infections, and their parents too. She could easily explain everything, her cocked head had seemed to say. So why had he not told her?

He fiddled with the oak banisters; traced the arches and curves with his index finger. How much did she guess? What did she know? He wanted so desperately to tell her everything: the nightmare of the air-raid shelter, the bleakness of the sea journey, the despair on Paddy's boyish face, the look of anguish when Jane hugged her child goodbye. He had tried to place a hand on Jane's shoulder in solidarity and her revulsion at his touch had sent shock waves down his spine. He had felt so alone.

When all was said and done, could he not trust Felicity with his desperate secret? "Felicity, forgive me! Be on my side!" he had wanted to say to her. But he had turned away and the moment had passed. There were residual feelings of jealousy always within him, and he had been frightened that she would leave him if she knew the part he had played in Tom's death.

"Go to bed!" Felicity said again.

Leaning heavily on the banisters he had climbed the stairs. On the landing he stumbled. How lovely it would be just to sit down there under his father's portrait and fall asleep, but then he would awaken surrounded by the pictures of his ancestors, some of whom were so righteous and solemn he could not have borne to see what would have seemed their reproachful eyes. The nightmares had started anyway. He was scared to sleep because it was a sleep traumatised by sounds of thudding bodies and tolling church bells.

He had shuffled on towards his room past the mahogany and gold-banded casket that stood near his bedroom door, a cherished possession, but now as he stood in front of it he was unable to feel the glow it ordinarily gave him. So much of him would never be the same again.

He showered and by the time he reached his bed supper had been brought to his room on a tray. Someone, probably Lucy, had drawn the thick, brocaded curtains across the balcony windows. Not a fleck of moonlight would penetrate these. The light above the bed scattered a subdued glow on the shiny rosewood cupboards. He left the door open into the little sitting room beyond. If Felicity would only come to him - oh the comfort of that thought - he longed to lie close beside her and wake up to find the whole monstrous thing a dream.

Later that night he heard Felicity go to her room; later still he heard her at his door and his heart beat fast. She moved about quietly; he saw her shadow run along the floor. When the room went dark he knew she had closed his door and gone away. He felt rejected. He should have called out to her, but he did not have the courage.

A stifled sneeze made him leave his bed. Pushing the curtains aside a full moon with puffs of creamy clouds beneath it beamed in upon him. Felicity stood near his window. She hardly looked at him but her body language welcomed him out to their shared balcony.

"Couldn't you sleep?" she asked, not looking at him, but waiting patiently for him to answer.

"No, I feel so restless. I seemed to drop off for a while but then I woke – I'm overtired."

"I'm sorry," she murmured, moving a little closer to him.

"Doesn't matter, I'll get plenty of sleep later." He leaned out over the balcony, his eyes boring into the dark, searching the distant bank bordering the garden, searching for reassurance. It was just the sort of night when a roam down the lawn would have calmed him - a badger-spotting night maybe, but just now he wanted to reach out to Felicity, and again his courage failed him.

Slowly the dawn appeared, breaking through the muslin curtain of night. Maurice felt soothed by her presence.

"I love this time," she said unexpectedly, moving her hand along the rail until her fingers and his were entwined.

"You don't seem to sleep much," he whispered to her, holding her fingers tightly between his own.

"If you want your dreams to come true, *don't sleep!*"

A faint sound drew his attention away from Felicity's words back to the lawn. Anna stood before them, lit by the early dawn; she disturbed the faint white mist that rose up from the grass as she advanced up the lawn making for the hall door. A bang and then fast footsteps up the stairs.

"Children *shouldn't be seen or heard.*" Felicity's voice was hard, then she laughed, "Don't be *a silly*, I'm joking."

***

Although the leaves were falling through the moist, early morning air and autumn was truly there, all day from late morning to the start of evening the sun shone and the afternoons were warm.

While Liadan lay on a rug to read, Anna joined her.

"I'll plait you hair," she offered.

Liadan could protest as much as she liked, her absorption in her book would not guard against Anna's determined attentions; Anna nudged her way onto the rug.

"Z for Zachariah, the best book ever," Anna tried to be normal. "What an off-putting name though," again she tried but Liadan continued to read.

Anna combed her hair into bunches, slowly and gently, hesitating now and then as if in mid thought, touching where the hair sprouted just above Liadan's ears, tickling her, making her squirm. Winding long strands through her fingers she pursed her lips in unspoken questions, until a little comfort seemed to come to her, flooding the dry knotted cords of anxiety that furrowed her brow. But Liadan felt the intrusion and it made her tetchy. She tried to move away from Anna without having to break off her reading. And in the end she shook her head, protesting loudly.

"Do you wonder what happened?" Anna asked the question Liadan dreaded the most.

Slamming her book closed, she moaned. No one only Anna asked her this type of question. People told her what she had seen, what she had felt; now she looked at Anna strangely frightened by the freedom this question gave her, and a little frightened at the intensity in Anna's face.

"I know what happened; I was there." They had gone over this so often, yet Anna continued to insist. Liadan returned to her book in an exaggerated manner, lifting it carefully and placing her finger strategically.

"No, what really happened?" Anna tugged her hair band, pretending an absorption in her hairdressing, but the tension throbbed visibly, her hand poised above Liadan's head in a question.

"You tell me, Anna, since you seem to know so much. You're so annoying; oh stop doing that!" She shook her head making her hair dance on her shoulders, unravelling the plaits as they bounced free.

"Did anyone die?"

"You mean did Paddy die?" Liadan shut her book again before answering her own question. " No!"

"But!"

"Everybody has told you...no Anna...no! You just won't listen. Will you? Paddy carried me back, remember?"

"Well?" Anna's lifeless voice went on.

"Well what?" Liadan's voice rose, "you're always asking the same questions. And then you say things like that... I've told you."

Anna sighed; she seemed distant, unaware of how anyone felt. Lucy said she just wanted to talk about Paddy. But Liadan knew her sister better. There was something else that she just would not ask and this thing was what she really wanted to know. Liadan was fed up with her. "You're getting very strange, you know that Anna?" she had pointed out.

"It doesn't matter anyway." Another of Anna's favourite declarations, and whereas often it had been a comfort to Liadan, today it inflamed her and she said crossly, shutting her book again for the umpteenth time:

"Why are you asking if it doesn't matter?" She rolled over trying to end the conversation. She brought her book right up close to her face.

"Am I the only one to see how everything's changed...It's like being in a different age or in some play where everyone is acting so badly... you, Daddy, everyone, you play-act as if things had not changed. The house is the same, the weather is hot, the donkey is unloving. Felicity, she's ...yes but I can see things, everything is going wrong. Oh it's good that you can't see what I see." Anna spoke in the strangest rush of words hardly allowing for a breath.

Liadan was speechless and she stared at Anna. And then the words tumbled out. "You're so boring Anna," she said "Can't you just forget it? You're always talking rubbish," and she ran into the house.

***

Some days later, like a playback, the same scenario was repeated over again with few changes. But then at the end Anna did not say that it didn't matter, she said: "I think you did see something. I think we're only allowed to know what's 'best for us' to know."

Liadan lay on her back looking up at the sky. She murmured in agreement.

"Do you think he's in the lake?" Anna asked.

"What sort of question is that?" Still Liadan turned over showing much more interest in this new question. "You don't mean Paddy again?"

Anna shook her head.

"You mean a body."

But Anna seemed to want to end the conversation.

"Nothing...never mind...nothing."

"No," Liadan insisted, "tell me!"

Lucy opened a bedroom window and leaning out shouted, "Get up off that damp grass! You'll get your deaths."

The cat appeared and stretched out between them, ignoring Lucy's advice. The sisters also ignored Lucy and continued their uneasy communication.

"When I look at him I just feel envy," Anna said, looking at the cat.

Liadan turned away, uninterested. Another conversation about the purpose of life was going to start, but she just wanted to play with the cat, daydream a bit and talk of school, her friends, even school work, anything but take the road of Anna's recent disenchantment. Liadan was too young to feel any adolescent yearning for melancholy and the change in her sister filled her with impatience and irritation.

"Nothing's wrong." Liadan said, trying to forestall Anna. She pushed her head into the soft fur of the cat's belly and the cat brought his paws down fiercely, gripping her head, before bounding off. Liadan laughed. She stretched in imitation of the cat and, getting on to her hands and feet, she tried to bound about until she fell over exhausted, crying out for Anna to laugh with her, to play with her. Why would she not be normal?

The trees were gold, red and orange - warm, dreamy colours. The hot days of summer would go on forever; wet dark winter was far away. Paddy had gone away but he would be back, Daddy had said so. There was nothing to worry about.

"Look...look Anna!"

The cat returned through the white grass, stalking them. He crept forward, waiting expectantly for the girls to charge.

Liadan looked encouragingly at Anna. She turned and saw a magpie:

"One for sorrow, two for joy..." she started to chant. Anna turned; her eyes were full of tears. The deep suffering in her sister's eyes frightened Liadan and she reacted with incomprehension and childish anger:

"Your hair smells," she offered in an aggrieved, sisterly way, "You pong, everyone says so."

She pushed Anna away from her, making room for the cat.

CHAPTER 13

Maurice rowed the boat past the shelter. Two months had gone by since he had buried Tom but because Anna sat by his side he felt an irresistible urge to row faster and his heart pounded. He understood that he had to control himself, so counting under his breath he kept a steady oar speed and, although Anna must have heard him mumble, she made no comment.

A lot of the vegetation surrounding the hillock had died away as winter approached. A group of young oak trees, just behind it, had lost their leaves and the needles of the larches standing by the pathway had turned to gold. Soon they too would fall, uncovering his favourite view of the house standing above.

The door to the showers came into sight and seemed in an odd way to invite further inspection. Anna turned her head.

"Let's go to the shelter," she said suddenly and shivered a little, "I haven't been in there for years."

Maurice's laugh was forced and false. He was surprised that Anna did not challenge him.

"Darling, you know it's dangerous." His strained voice was falsetto but she did not seem to notice that either.

"I know." Already her voice had lost its tremor of excitement.

"I had to lock the old kitchen door. I'm afraid the roof timbers are rotten... we can have a quick look later, if you want." His voice relaxed as he talked and sounded almost normal. Anna had gradually seemed to lose interest in the things around her, but she still asked unexpected, probing questions while very quickly desisting and giving up at the first resistance: it was as though she did not want to persist and did not really want to know.

Already the laurel bushes that Maurice had planted around the entrance had established themselves; each year they would grow larger. There were wild fuchsia and a bank of nettles in the summer months, and around the dome of the shelter thick brambles like crooked arms criss-crossed, creating a crown of thorns. No one would be tempted to climb up above the shelter; he had planted holly, white thorn trees and leylandii here and there just to fill in any empty spaces.

The overcast sky hung low over the lake. Early that morning there had been a downpour and any prospect of brightness was distant, with the sky filling slowly and building towards a much more prolonged deluge. Some of the birds did not even seem to be aware that morning had arrived; they sat listlessly on silver birch branches puffing out their feathers and silently surveying the boat beneath.

Maurice felt the heaviness of Anna's heart and he struggled, digging deep, to find a cheerful word that would not suggest that he had any fault to find in her sadness. She missed Paddy, but there was no point in him saying so, because she would only deny it. Covertly he watched her as she leaned back in her seat; her face, so often a riot of emotion, looked gaunt and dull. Her eyes, large and pain-filled, were bordered with dark, smudged, blue-brown circles, like some comic painting of an insomniac. An arm lay uncomfortably on the back of the boat with a wrist so thin the tiny bones could be counted; the sight of them pierced his heart with pain. Oh Anna, when would she be the old Anna again?

Why she had wanted to go to the shelter, he did not understand: he did not believe that she could have any inkling of what had happened. He knew that she had had no contact with Paddy subsequent to that dreadful day, but this was the first time in a long while that she had seemed to be interested in something external to herself. He knew that she was with him in the boat only to placate him, to stop his questions, to get away from Wendy's cloying sympathy. Anna had never had the inclination to reject or spurn anyone; it was not in her nature and now anyway she appeared unable to respond either positively or negatively to the importuning of her family and friends. Any opportunity that presented itself to escape the constant and often silent interrogation of those around her, she grasped gratefully and her father was not now surprised at her presence beside him in the boat. Although he was one of those who wished deeply to know her troubles and to help her, he was more prepared to wait and more prepared to suffer in silence the long and lugubrious unhappiness of his daughter.

"Those ducks should have gone by now. It'll be quite a relief to see them go... they dirty the water. Next year they'll be back. That's the way of the world," he laughed pathetically. "See Anna," but how could he talk to this emaciated stranger? How she looked at him with dead eyes. Her silence dried his mouth. "They'll be back."

She glanced over to where a group of six ducks moved up and down by the reed stems. They drove their heads into the water one by one, popping their bottoms up; the full-grown babies and mother were now indistinguishable.

They continued to the northern-most point of the lake before he spoke again.

"We were wondering if you'd any plans? You had so many different ideas; Felicity thought you might try your hand at design... fabrics, she thought. Don't ask me..." He laughed in an encouraging way, looking at her again, seeking some response but none came. She hardly moved; the only signs of life were a tiny throb below her jawbone and the quick pulse of movement as she swallowed.

"Of course, if you've some other idea that would also be good. Liadan said you wanted to go to Italy?" He took a deep breath, letting it out in a sigh. Again nothing.

He felt an urgency to think of something else to say or do and in the end he exclaimed enthusiastically, "You don't mind if I try my luck here?" lifting his fishing bag from the bottom of the boat. Searching for inspiration, he looked out over the water and then down the length of his rod to the tip which seemed to be resting on the surface. He flicked the fly into the water, but a restlessness made him want to move on and he took the oars into his hands again. Manoeuvring the boat around, he set out west to an open area, not shrouded by bushes and trees. Here the lake became deep, even very close to the shore. A heron swooped down to feed but spotting them regained the sky, flapping loudly. Maurice took his time casting out his line, away from the boat, into the dark depths. It made a pinging sound and rings of water sped away.

His thoughts were rushed and his mind was crowded with things that he might say but he tried to keep his movements calm and to appear engrossed in what he was doing. The rod bounced in his hands and the spinner bobbed and moments later he gently reeled in a small red-finned silver fish.

"Pass me the net!" he asked, all business-like, and Anna reached forward with it, helping him to slip the net in under the struggling fish. He felt her tears before he saw them.

"What's the matter Anna? Come on... talk to me, I can help. It can't be that bad surely? There's nothing to be worried about. Whatever is wrong ...just tell me... you have to tell me."

"Let it go, Daddy" she said.

As he did her bidding, he said gently. "I want you to believe me no matter what is troubling you ...we can help...please darling, let me help."

He took her hand and pulled her to his side and the boat settled and drifted. Without a wind the lake looked untroubled, occasional fish surfaced drawing Maurice's eye. He kept looking into the distance hoping that she might find it easier to speak to him if he did not look at her directly. The boat moved into a blanket of warm moist air. The sky was yellow away from the heavy mists that circled the lake.

"I'm not the sort of father to let you down."

A blackbird gave a warning call, clipped, sudden and apprehensive. In the boat the silence continued. She sat close but apart from him, only allowing her arm to touch his.

"I wouldn't let you down," he said again and his voice conveyed such emotion that she pushed her hand into his and her head fell on his arm. He waited for her to speak but she seemed unable to do so.

"What is it," he asked in desperation. "Is it Paddy?"

Her head turned away from him and she said so timidly, "Nothing will be the same," that later he wondered if he had heard her correctly.

"Oh is this really all...why, at your age, should you want anything to be the same? Come on Anna! Paddy will come back and even if he had never gone away things would have changed! You're young, you're beautiful, enjoy your life!" He felt a burst of relief. He nudged her gently with his shoulder, smiling down at her in an encouraging way. As Felicity suspected, nothing too serious seemed to be the problem: just Paddy, and some other adolescent nonsense. She might have seemed "too old" to other people, but to him she was his little girl. The relief he felt welled up in him and he looked at her with more impatience than understanding.

But the little girl on his arm would not, could not, pull herself together. She looked even more unhappy: as though she now knew that there would never be any salvation, never be any discernment or comprehension of her plight. She was alone, not because others did not want to understand, but because they could not.

"I wish I'd never been born," she said firmly but not in the slightest accusingly.

Her words stung: "How can you be so ungrateful," he stormed, emphasizing this dreadful incomprehension of the bleak and untenanted world where she found herself.: "How can you be so selfish ...you are lucky to be given life... to be born," he shouted, his evangelical fervour taking over. To him her reaction was at least a reaction: she had finally stirred herself; he now had something to go on, even if it were confrontational.

Anna stared at him in astonishment; he saw the question in her face: "How could she talk to him?" She slipped her hand away from his and he knew too late that he had let himself down. Nothing he could say would retrieve the damage his words had done. Her eyes filled with hopelessness; nothing he said would be of any use. But he had to try to make her see:

"Darling," he said, "Paddy had to go." His voice shook with the memory. "A terrible thing happened: a terrible accident. Paddy had to go: he hit his father. Tom had a heart attack and died. It looked so bad for Paddy…but he's alive and well. Do you see, darling?" he asked, "He didn't mean it. We had to keep it secret. I wanted…what?" He stammered.

Anna was laughing, yet not laughing. The anguish in her face hurt him. She clutched her chest.

"Oh Daddy now I understand. Why didn't you tell me?" She laughed again. "Now I understand …he did love me…he didn't leave me."

***

All that morning they had looked for her. It had been a beautiful morning; a morning which endowed even the most unfavoured corners of the countryside with loveliness, inducing a feeling of security, of warmth and contentment, distancing any possibility of destruction or distress. Later when Felicity checked her room, her bed had not been slept in. Even then, not once in his anxiety that she should be found had he suspected her fate. Looking back, who could have foreseen the extremes of that day: a morning of pure serenity and then the horror that was to come? They had searched the house. Anna's room, so untidy most days, was spick and span. As usual her window was open to the elements, curtain-less, except for the lightest of white muslin that floated on the air. Honeysuckle crept through the opening, dormant at the beginning of winter. Moths and bugs had crawled in behind the stems to hibernate. Anna could never object to any of them. Anna should have lived in a jungle, everyone said. Above her black-leaded fireplace, on a mantelpiece of grass-green inlaid tiling, stood her most treasured possessions: miniature portraits and pink translucent seashells. Over a silver mirror and circling the walls of the room Anna had sketched little pictures of butterflies.

"She's so clever," Maurice said, as he always said whenever he visited her room. Shrewdly he shied away from close examination, suspecting that some of the butterflies had faces not unlike his own - Anna's wicked sense of humour. Even at this moment he could smile with pride, but to Felicity there was nothing much to smile about in that room.

"Yes, *clever, but this is all quite ridiculous*" Felicity had snapped before leaving as Lucy arrived.

"And we know what we think of the likes o' her..." Lucy said to her back.

"Now what?" Maurice asked. "What's she done?"

"She should leave the girls alone. There, I've said my bit."

"Nonsense! Anna's very difficult just now and where is she, that's what I'd like to know."

"As I said, I've said my bit."

Anna and Felicity had not seen eye to eye of late, Maurice knew. Anna's wild ways and her even wilder room, where the seasons became a part of her sleeping experience, were not acceptable to Felicity.

"I want to feel things," Anna had said to Felicity when asked to shut her window, "I like to feel cold," she had laughed at Felicity's uncomprehending face. "I could sleep outside. I would be fine"

"You're a funny girl," Felicity had said with almost a touch of warmth in her voice, "and a *wild one*." Even though Felicity could not understand, she did feel that it might be an answer to the problem of Anna's room and the damage that she felt Anna's ways were causing to the house, and she would have been quite happy to give Anna her head about sleeping outside; however, she knew Maurice would not want his daughter expelled to the garden.

"We'll put up some netting...*to stop the birds* from coming in. Beautiful things are more important than *anything*, they're not dispensable artefacts - not in *my book*." Felicity's voice was squeaky with raw emotion. "*Really darling* no more birds... please. *How can you allow beautiful things to be destroyed?* "

"I won't..." Anna agreed.

Lately they had avoided each other.

"I've made her cross again," he had heard Anna tell Liadan, but he'd taken no notice, poor Anna was not herself.

***

Anna's head popped up like a cork breaking the brown water , sending waves off into the reeds, her face turned towards the sky, as if for one last look, then disappearing again beneath the surface. Maurice rushed to the lake's edge when he saw her, tearing at his clothes, ripping them from his body, letting out a howling sound. He threw himself into the water and swimming strongly reached her quickly, but she had already been dead for some time. Her legs were plaited tightly together with reeds and the dark large flowers were still attached to her body as he dragged her to the bank. Already there was something putrid about his darling Anna; his horrified eyes warned him. Her skin was swollen and slimy and he felt afraid of that lifeless face and those white pupil-less eyes. His diaphragm pushing up into his rib cage allowed him only occasional loud gasps and tortured cries. When at last the spasm passed he lay down beside her. He could not leave her, gathering her into his arms he held her close to his breast. He lay with her for a minute... or an hour. Everything was dead around him. He looked with disbelief at the ugly cedars and the black lake before him.

How much time had passed, he could not tell, it was late in the afternoon and the sun was going down. It sat surrounded by a dark rain cloud sparkling like an enormous diamond. Maurice could not understand where he was, what had happened, where he had been. He looked up from under his thick, swollen eyelids and he saw his Anna coming out of the blue lake. She rose from the water and moved to the bank. Her arms reached forward towards a light. Her face radiant she smiled in his direction but apparently without seeing him, and he thought he could see yellow butterflies dancing around her head in a soft and flimsy halo. He tried to reach out to her; he tried to call to her but she faded quickly away.

CHAPTER 14

Years later I bumped into Jane in Templeslaney. She told me Paddy would be coming home. Bitterly I spoke out before thinking.
"Over my dead body." I said.
"That could be arranged." She laughed in such a hideous way she made me shudder a little. I believe she has it in her.

***

Like many another town in Ireland, with their Market Squares and their Irish Streets, Templeslaney had its own large river; a river ebbing and flowing cutting deep a valley which served so well as a setting for a town. For what is any town without a river running through it, without "quays" and neglected warehouses. The river in Templeslaney divided the town in two and the two sides rose sharply up from it. On a height above the Market Square the Pugin cathedral stretched out its wings like a mother swan gathering in her cygnets. Though surrounded by commercial activities it held itself aloof behind a stout wall; tombstones leaned this way and that on grassy banks. In the distance the Blackstairs Mountains faded to dried lavender blue.

***

Maurice made his way over the bridge. He had left his car in the car park at the back of the hotel which fronted on to the bridge and as he walked he contemplated the old arch that he was crossing. The bridge, he thought was the logical centre of the town. He remembered seeing, in the various trivial investigations that he had made with regard to the town, some old prints which gave pride of place to the bridge that he was crossing.

Now it was the natural repair of the unemployed who could sit on the wall and gaze down into the water as they reviewed the events of the day or week. Maurice loved the town; he loved its people and he loved to think at length about them and their town and its interconnections with the countryside and the life that he lived. He looked over the wall of the bridge down into the river; if one gazed hard enough, and the time of year was right, one could see the salmon making their way up, for the river was famous for its salmon.

***

Jane mouthed something that seemed like an obscenity from lips coated in the same bruise-coloured lipstick he remembered of old. Her words spun around in his head. Her unblinking eyes tracked him. She would have been conspicuous in any gathering; by the 1798 commemorative statue she was clearly visible. She had grown thin and the darkness of her skin and hair seemed to be more intense. None of her natural physical presence was lost in her premature ageing and when Maurice saw her he was covered with intense dread, as if she were an evil forewarning of some great catastrophe. Nothing relieved the dark nature of her aspect: her face was deeply morbid and her clothing like a nun's habit, missing only a veil. Her bony fingers flashed a horrid purple varnish. Finding her eyes fixed upon him made him nervous. It was bad luck that he had met her that day. She was talking and her words to him were like a blow making his knees buckle. His hand reached out to steady himself.

"Paddy didn't think any such thing, you crazy witch." Maurice spluttered.

"Nothing would have made me agree to your arrangements," she pointed out coldly, "only the truth of what I'm telling you. You're a stupid man."

"No. You're lying," he fumed and shook.

"Why else would I have allowed Paddy to take the consequences of your acts? Do you think anyone would believe him innocent, knowing what we knew and knowing what you would say?"

Her awful words held him transfixed.

At midday the people of the town spilled out into the streets, milling around, doing their business in a frenetic lunch-hour rush. Delia Collins, the pharmacist, saw them not far from her door and came from her shop to speak to Jane, her presence immediately returning things to normal.

"It's lovely to see you, Jane. Sure where have you been? We'd hoped you'd come back and spend most of the summer here. You used to find the time for us!" Delia chuckled.

From the top of her head down to her red toes Delia shook and trembled, her laughter bubbling over. She had big soft eyes in a big soft face and because she loved ice-cream the fatness extended all over her person. Even in a blizzard Delia would have left her chemist shop to cross the square to Brian Hanley for his home-made rum and raisin ice-cream.

Jane smiled and startled Maurice: her face became sweet. He had seen faces change with happy news but Jane's face turned in a moment from granite to a face filled with light. Why, before all that had happened, could not she have smiled like that at him? He would have responded and they might have been friends; he had done nothing then to upset her.

Delia chuckled excitedly and he stood by as they talked, somehow unable to leave.

"How's Felicity?" Delia asked him eventually.

"Fine, thanks. She's busy as always!" Maurice tried to concentrate on Delia's question. "She's arranging for Liadan to spend next summer in France, we thought perhaps Liadan should finish her schooling there. It might help her to get away for a while. They've been over there the last few weeks trying to find the right area. Only arrived back last night."

"My goodness, what age is she? I wouldn't have thought her old enough!"

"Fifteen. Yes, she's growing up. It's been so difficult for her."

As he spoke he wanted to glare at Jane; to pinpoint the blame where the blame should be. But Jane had returned to stone; he felt defeated.

Delia, the soul of discretion, seemed to understand they were straying on to dangerous ground. "It's always nice to cut the reins, get away!" she burst out and blushed.

Maurice revived somewhat: people in the town thought Tom had run out on Jane and he knew Delia was thinking that too. "Yes it is," he said. "Who wants to stay stuck in a rut?" He smiled maliciously at Jane. "She'll spend a large portion of her time visiting art galleries; she's studying the history of art as her main subject and French Literature."

"Oh my! She'll be so cultured." Delia exclaimed, a delighted smile spreading over her face. "A lovely girl, Liadan."

Maurice glowed. "Very kind of you! Well, I must be off, I'm afraid."

Delia chuckled, "This square is a magnet... I'm sure we'll be bumping into each other." She chuckled some more at the thought of it.. "Call in any time, won't you?."

Jane hardly seemed to notice when he left and he muttered something civil to her as he went. He could hear Delia bring up the subject of the bypass - the town's safe subject of conversation.

He needed to buy a gate; he needed to order crop seed and a couple of bags of oats that he would stick in the boot of his car for his horses and the old donkey. But most of all he needed his lunch. He would not think again of what mad Jane had said. No one need know.

***

That afternoon Maurice sat in his study staring out into the rain; large tears crept down his face. He did not want to believe; he could not. He would never, ever believe such a thing. His green desk drawers were sticking as usual, but the memories of Liadan and her games could not distract him from his melancholy. The rain beat incessantly against the panes, running down the window so that the glass seemed to take on a belligerent life of its own.

Felicity came into the room with new curtains and Maurice rose to help her. Rich, dark, red-brocaded curtains that would brighten up his study, she said, and as each curtain fell into place a red glow was reflected in the glass, smudging in the watery windowpanes. Felicity spoke to Maurice as she would to a helpless child:

"Jane told you the *truth*."

"No, No! don't … It can't be…you never said before."

"How *could* I? Anyway you *wouldn't have* believed me… not then. Not now by *the looks of things*." Her chin lifted up, "Forget it …*get on* with things."

More tears fell.

"Why tell me now?" he asked angrily.

"Last night you were calling in your sleep…you begged for forgiveness…*would you now*? No… maybe you'll sleep better tonight." Felicity's voice was cold, "Every night with*out fail*… It can't go on."

She should have been quiet like she usually was. Felicity did not know everything. The moment she closed the door behind her, Maurice turned again to the window. Loud sobs filled the room. He filled his glass.

* * *

Paddy never wrote to Anna, not once over those months. He could have done that.

If for any reason Tom's remains are found you will have to let the authorities know that Tom's death was an accident.

My Darling, I hope with all my heart you don't have to and that you can put it behind you and get on with your life.

Take care of yourself, my Lia darling! You are the world to me.

Daddy.
Signed: Maurice Agan
Witnessed: Sean Dalkey, Solicitor.

***

After dinner, that same evening, Maurice called at Seals. This old pub, just off the Market Square was his favourite, being dark and neglected; few women ever went to drink there. It had deep Burgundy-coloured walls with floors of slate and stone and every night an open fire to welcome the customer. Iron pots and hanging skewers, parts of ploughs and single cartwheels hung along the uneven walls. The rough tables were cleaned and the fire set each day, but webs hung from the ceiling rafters forming an intricate canopy above the drinkers. Seats were felt to be owned by right of regularity. But Maurice chose to sit where he wanted and people were polite enough not to fuss. He knew them all. He was a man of the people, he would say to himself, liking to share the company of the strong farmers of the district as well as the humble postman. On this night he did not feel like bothering much with conversation or any of the people present.

Samuel Seal leaned forward doing a cleaning motion with his arm. He looked expectantly at Maurice. He was about Maurice's age and they had known each other from childhood. Who could tell if Samuel liked Maurice: no one knew whom Samuel liked, not even his wife. Samuel looked dwarfed in Maurice's presence, in stature, in status and in affluence.

"What's it going to be, BC?" Samuel asked and Maurice smiled. Everyone got called BC in Samuel's pub. He claimed it stood for "Best Customer."

"A whiskey please, Samuel, no water." Maurice answered.

He leaned back against the bar and surveyed the group, draining his glass at the same time. Although it was early in the evening already some were getting animated about the bypass. He screwed his face up in response to the hearty drink he had taken and the topic of conversation. Though he had taken the trouble to make sure it would not affect his land months ago, he worried that public outcry would mean adjustments to the direction of the road. Why did these people not leave the topic alone? What they were suggesting would mean ruin for him. Who would choose to put a bypass there? Not being the sort of man to contain himself he took another whiskey from Samuel and walked over to join in the conversation.

"This is pure hair-brained rubbish," he said with a slightly raised voice, his face red from the whiskey and red from his ill humour. "Besides the river cuts into the path of your bypass and who in their right minds would choose bridge-building when a bypass going from Garrow to Cluainbeg would be more direct and have no need of a fancy bridge? I say it's madness." He drank his whiskey again in one gulp.

Adrian O'Connor looked smug and knowing and, being only a junior in the Co Council offices, everyone knew that the information he freely gave was affected by a certain inventiveness. Yet today he held many ears.

"I saw a plan for two bypasses that will merge about ten miles south of the town, " He said

"Nonsense... madness... can't believe that!" Maurice said swallowing his third whiskey." He smiled indulgently at Adrian. He could not ever get a story straight or have any real insight about anything, Maurice thought. Aloud he said: "But I will believe anything if I'm reincarnated as a donkey".

Everyone laughed, even Adrian.

"I know what I've seen," Adrian muttered.

"Well, we are all worried" Samuel said. He did not want the conversation to dry up, else their drinking would stop and they would talk of going home.

"I don't think they have decided just yet what we will get and to be honest I wonder if we are ready for a bypass. Trade is bound to suffer," Peter Yates put in.

Maurice drained his glass a fourth time. A quick circle with his finger galvanised Samuel into supplying all present with further sustenance. Maurice was in form and Samuel forecast a very good night's takings.

***

When Maurice emerged from Seals several hours later the night was quiet and the clouds were tinged with pink by the lights of the urban area; they trailed across the sky and the moon made an occasional appearance, lighting some areas and creating pools of darkness. Already the town had grown still. The trekking to nightclubs twenty miles to the south had taken all the young away. Maurice stretched at the pub door, took two erratic steps and decided he should walk home. By the time he got there he would be stone sober and able to look Felicity in the face. As time had gone by, and he drank more and more, he was less and less able to prevent his wife or daughter from finding him drunk. Trying to keep anything from Liadan was impossible. These kids, he thought, never seemed to want their beds at night and then when morning came where would you find them? He had tried everything to entice her to get up early. He rolled a little, just managing to regain his balance. A car sounded its horn and he waved his hand acknowledging their "greeting or warning or whatever", he thought to himself, and swayed a bit more. By the time he had reached the top of the town an hour had passed. He sat on a wall watching the lights flicker and go out as Templeslaney's citizens made their way to bed. The road that he had taken had the history of the people in its foundation; their very bones might even be a part of it and when Maurice drove down to town or when returning he would remember that different time, when gangs of hungry men had hewn out the rock a century ago. He imagined himself part of that group, hacking at the rock, pick-axing out the boulders and with bare hands dragging them, pushing them, digging down deep into the rock of their being as they dug down deep into the ground, moving what must have seemed like heaven and earth just for a bowl of porridge. Thinking of that work that they had had to do made him catch his breath, made his eyes wet.

Suddenly he felt tired and he had still some way to go. If he did not hurry, it would be morning and the house would be waking up. He would be caught red-handed and even though it was unlikely that Felicity would confront him or that Liadan would be around, he was sick of the feeling of shame and guilt that his uncontrolled drinking always gave him. Forget all that, he told himself. Maybe, he thought childishly, he'd show them he still had a sense of humour, he would play a joke on Liadan and creep to her room, bang on her door and trick her into getting up before dawn. But Liadan had grown up. To be honest, he thought to himself, he had never managed to get her up before she was ready. She would be so angry if he tried.

On the long road home he had ample time to reflect. He thought about all the recent happenings, about his girls, Anna and Liadan …about Felicity. That very afternoon he had finished the letter; all other business was completed with the solicitor, Dalkey. There would be no need for Jane to make any statements. He had kept his promise to her about that. Sometimes, he mused, it was better to stick to vague generalisations than the ABC of actual happenings. Doing things for the best rather than fussing about concepts of pristine truth was more important for a father.

The dark avenue drew him on into its tunnel of trees. The moon was now bright in the autumn night sky; the clouds had cleared and the avenue was lit up where there was a break in the trees or a gate-way into a field. At one of these openings Maurice stood peering into the gloom, knowing each rise and fall of the land, each bush and bank. The sheep would be settled underneath the horse-chestnut trees by the top gate and he knew that remaining for a while leaning on the gate would not disturb them. Maurice liked to have a contented flock. He would have been a good shepherd if he had come from humble stock: a contented, diligent herdsman. As he mused on his own finer qualities he became aware of an unpleasant musky odour. Now alert to any sound, he heard the soft pad of feet close by.

"Good evening, Mr Fox," he whispered.

A few moments later he heard the sheep moving restlessly and he knew the fox had passed them by. Then an eerie cry went up from the further corner of the field, by a small coppice.

"It's the banshee," he sighed.

**

Next morning they found Maurice's cold body, his clothes damp from the morning dew. One side of his face was blackened where the blood had hardened.

There was no need to cut Maurice's wrists. He was decidedly dead, and although Felicity knew this, she had promised him she would.

"He was terrified, you know love." Lucy took Liadan out of the room. She hushed Liadan's hysterical crying. "He was terrified of being buried alive. He suffered horribly from a recurring dream...nothing for you to worry about, my goodness, nothing at all. Some people get a bit funny," she said dismissing both Felicity and Maurice. Liadan and she were now the only ones left.

Chapter 15

Wendy came down from the lover's gate waving her arms and lifting her knees in a vain attempt at running. "Isn't that enough for today?" she called.

Liadan swam to the bank. She loved her swims; she loved the way the bank was overgrown with buttercups; she dried herself on her t-shirt in a perfunctory way before pulling it over her head, pressing it to her nose. Yellow irises grew in profusion along the edge of the lake; the seductive scent clung to her body and t-shirt.

"Um... nice," Wendy sniffed the air. She seemed pleased with herself.

The girls walked along saying little to each other until they stood on the south bank where the beech trees grew and the grass was lumpy underfoot from the beech mast.

"I dreamt last night about falling over..." Liadan said. She was talking more to herself than to Wendy. Wendy was not her confidante; she was a human presence here in the place where the action, which to Liadan was both real and imaginary, had taken place and which now in a momentary way made Liadan want to talk.

Trees being felled in the distance burst in on her words reminding her of the sounds in her dreams: the loud thud of men fighting, the sharp sound of voices warning.

"Oh Lia, I don't think..." A pale tide washed over Wendy's face. She held her breath under the strain of wanting to know but feeling she ought not to ask. Liadan watched her with cold eyes; irritated, she turned away to look across the lake to where the giant bull rushes' thick brown stalks grew on the water's edge. Anna and the bull rushes had somehow become almost synonymous to Liadan, because one always reminded her of the other. Wendy would not want to hear talk like that. Liadan decided that anyway she had no intention of telling Wendy what she had dreamt: she was ignorant and would stay ignorant.

As was so often the case when Wendy came to stay they talked and talked of everything, except the one thing Liadan wanted to talk about: the subject Wendy could not face, and must not know about. Wendy would freak out if she knew that close by Tom was buried. Again a tree fell in the distance and Liadan's mind wandered to her dream and the voices she had heard coming through the darkness.

***

"Lies... liar … you gobshite," she heard her father shouting again and again; a forbidden word; a word he said he hated. It was so like him to say one thing and do another, but she did not blame him at all. Tom had taunted him. She could remember the feeling of his words and when she was dreaming, she understood them, but that clarity would disappear on waking. Only the feeling of livid outrage against Tom remained.

***

"I saw Ronan this morning; he said you hadn't returned his call. He wants to see you, Lia. Why are you being so mean to him?" Wendy teased making a face.

Liadan caught bits and pieces of what Wendy was saying and she smiled; she was mean. She would call him. She drifted into her thoughts again.

"You know Paddy was home."

The name made Liadan's heart pound.

"What?" She stopped walking, she was all attention: "Honestly you're so annoying…why didn't you tell me immediately…"

And before Wendy could even begin, Liadan interrupted.

"About Paddy, of course."

"Oh, there's nothing much to say. He was staying with his uncle a couple of weeks ago. He's gone back to Kenya now, but

people say he's coming back for good. And..." Wendy took
ages, "Ciarán saw him, he said he'd changed a lot; you wouldn't
recognise him."

"Why?"

"He's like a skeleton and ..." Wendy seemed meditative; Liadan flared up with impatience; she found Wendy's measured
and deliberate way of giving information exasperating; why
could she not get on with it?

"And *what*?"

"Unkempt. She says he's like a dropout. Can you imagine?"

Liadan laughed "*Dropout...* poor Pads! It'll be great to have
him back again." No, she did not hold anything against Paddy,
no matter what her father said.

The thought of Paddy returning for good kept Liadan happy.
Once again she felt the warmth of his existence. And though
she encouraged Ronan, in her heart she knew her love was elsewhere. She never spoke to Ronan of Paddy, but she did of everything else for she found him very easy to talk to. She did not
want to lose his friendship now that they had become friends.
The one thing she ought to have done she could not bring herself to do and that was to analyse her feelings for Paddy. How
could she? She would have had to say: "I was 11 years old and
had a crush on him; still do, even though I have not seen him
for 8 years. He was my sister's boyfriend and now I think he
belongs to me."

***

"No one has the right to destroy the lake," she said to Ronan,
"not for a stupid road anyway. What I said before about leaving
Templeslaney won't happen. I'm now much more determined to
stay."

"Of course! It's your home; anybody can understand that."
Ronan looked pathetically pleased.

"It's as though we were becoming extinct: all my real family are gone…no close relatives…" Her mood was sombre but she smiled, "I need to be here… all a bit mad."

"No, it's not and you're not alone. You'll marry and…"

She laughed, "OK, OK!"

She hated to think she was being a bit underhand in getting his sympathy and his help, but the fear of what might be found should the road gobble up the shelter grew daily. It was a strong enough motivation for her. She could not get the dread of discovery out of her head.

Most Saturday afternoons from early September through to December Liadan and Ronan met in the library overlooking the square, their mission being to save the lake, to find some way to stop the road. Each in turn excited the other with unrealistic scenarios, but they were always close to admitting defeat. They had moved backwards and forwards over the same ground many times without advancing an inch. Stalemate loomed large. Liadan could not imagine how she would face the outcry when the truth was known. Ronan was desperately sorry for her. He did not know her real reason. He believed that her determined attempts to stave off what seemed inevitable had to do with her memories; memories which for him were also very active, but could not compare with her wish to keep untouched the things that had surrounded her sister and her father and on which they had left an indelible mark. He understood her desperation, or thought he did: how could she allow some of the most poignant and intense scenes of her childhood to be destroyed and erased forever by tarmacadam.

"Your neighbours, the Fitzwilliams, were new to the area and don't live here now, why couldn't the road go through their property? It's got no history. Who would care? I heard they were selling up anyway?" He shrugged.

She stepped forward to look closer, not expecting much.

"Oh no! It's no good… " he went on "If the road went that way it would be very near the house on the west side." He moved away.

"Wait a minute." Liadan leant forward. "Oh Ronan! It could work; it could save Tuskar's lake. It's passing Garrvine hill on the east, so why not?" Her finger shook over the map and her voice became strained with excitement. "Do you see?" She laughed out, loud placing her finger over her lips to suppress herself. "You're brilliant!" she whispered. She threw her arms around his neck and kissed him.

"But Lia, it would be closer to the house and a lot of land would be lost." Ronan said. He held her, not allowing her to escape. His eyes had become narrow and dark.

"No, no, it's good," she smiled, giving in to his arms and then gently and kindly releasing herself.

Before the worry of the shelter, she knew she would have rejected such a suggestion. No wonder Ronan looked puzzled, but then how could he understand. She supposed Paddy would understand very well and he would have to talk to his mother. Knowing about the body changed everything: the excessive loss of land to save the lake could not have been considered before, but now everything was different. It had not entered her head until Ronan had suggested this new route, that making such a sacrifice would remove the danger. Liadan laughed with relief. She looked at the map again. Ronan quickly drew a line across the map that to her seemed more direct than the official line. Their heads touched as they leant over the table and she turned towards him touching his cheek. Ronan's pencilled line swept the Fitzwilliam's house and gardens aside, took some of the best land at Tuskar and came into view on the southwest of the house. They could live with that if Jane had no objection. She might even be cajoled into actual canvassing on their behalf. This Liadan felt sure would make the tide of events turn in their favour; surely Jane would not want his body to be found after all this time. Liadan shivered a little.

"We'll ask Felicity," Liadan said, "she'll know. The Johnsons, Paddy's relatives, are her friends and have political pull, a hold on the *powers that be*". Liadan mimicked Felicity repeating *"powers that be"* pursing her lips and forming the words sometimes in a precise, clipped and shortened manner, sometimes drawn out into a drawl. Ronan stooped to kiss her softly, caressing her chin.

Before reason could prevail Liadan felt the thrill of his kiss. She looked at him shyly. No! This could not be: it was not him she wanted. Yet her heart did race and she again noticed his eyes and how his lean face had grown handsome.

"Felicity knows the Fitzwilliams well, maybe she should speak to Tom," Ronan said, "Do they know where he is now?"

With a shaky voice Liadan replied, "Oh they know alright, but I don't think they'd want to. Best if she speaks to Paddy."

She tried to sound a bit ironical without too much emphasis.

The kiss passed without comment, seeming almost to have been forgotten.

An icy wind from the north blew fluffy snow clouds over the distant mountains and down onto the plain; the light dusting of crystal snow left behind lay on top of each windowsill, shimmering like tiny stars. The town looked newly washed in yellow light and the shade around the buildings grew deep. The sun, low in the sky, gave little warmth and appeared only partially from behind the heavy snow clouds. Looking from the library window, out past the square and down the street, Liadan could see the river below cutting the town in two: on this side, the castle on the right and the cathedral on the left defined the outer margins of her visual field. Up until recently she had wanted to be in a city surrounded by life, not scratching in a backwater at a problem already past solving. If she looked out of the window long enough perhaps Phil might walk by and have a chat with Mick who was buying a paper or hungry Delia would crunch across the snow for her ice cream: in these little events would lie the excitement for the day. Liadan placed her chin upon her hand and waited. Today was different. Everything was happening. There was hope. Ronan was sweet. The kiss was gratifying. He was clever and good-looking. His love-filled eyes were greeny-blue with a black fleck and she thought she would like to look into them again. Hurriedly she turned to look out on to the square, pressing her warm forehead against the icy pane of glass. They were so high up above the town, almost as though they were standing on a platform. One could look straight down the narrow street to the café and the cotton tree. In summer the tree looked as if snow clouds were sitting upon its branches, with occasional fluffy snow balls dropping on to the town's new brides and grooms embracing for their wedding photographs under its white umbrella. The burnt-out hotel beyond the river looked newly built in this fading light. Liadan sat back away from the window. She lingered a little continuing to think about the town and, like her father, to consider what it had always meant to her, its associations, communications and connections with her life: even when she had been away and walked through other towns and shopped in other shops, she had always kept it there, stored in her memory, ready to be viewed and reviewed in quiet moments. She remembered the hotel before it had been burnt and she remembered how she had felt a certain desolation on hearing that it was gone.

Now she had an urge to throw her maps into the air, to shout out loud.

"Shall we go to the café?" she asked instead, gathering up the papers.

The streets that they walked down from the library to the café were deserted. There were large lengths of pathway cleared of ice and other darker areas with perilous iced-over puddles. They clung to each other in mock fear, laughing loudly, slipping as they went. Yellow lights lit the Garda headquarters and the street beyond, creating pools of brightness and darkness; shadows flitted across them as they made their way down Slaney Street. The narrow, steep street allowed very little of the intemperate weather to enter and seemed almost to have its own micro-climate. The river at the bottom of the street flowed full with black water in from a rough sea. Three days earlier, before the snow had arrived, a gale had stirred up the water, so that it splashed and crashed its way inland.

Liadan's thoughts drifted lightly here and there. A sudden sadness was quickly replaced by nervous laughter when Ronan fell over at the café door.

The aroma of baked cakes and coffee wafted out to them from the café, lifting their spirits and making them rowdy and loud as they pushed open the door into the dark corridor, bringing the cold air in with them.

Sylvia, the café owner spotted Liadan and Ronan straight away and rushed to the counter to take their order. Her tone was a mix of subservience and familiarity. She made enquiries as to how Liadan was and what she would like to eat and drink, but her voice and bearing were to Liadan only a masquerade of sincerity.

"How's it going?" Sylvia asked, "What's it to be?" She lifted the coffee pot expectantly and smiled awkwardly.

Liadan suspected that Sylvia did not like her.

"We all thought you stuck-up before we got to know you properly." Kitty, Sylvia's daughter, had told her.

So Liadan, surmising with the help of Kitty's rash comments, gave expression to Sylvia's thoughts about her: "This young one has it all. Some people have to work for a living. They are a stuck-up lot and this one is the most difficult of them."

Sylvia's eyes were hard, although her lips formed a smile. She turned to speak to Ronan.

"Ronan, a chara, how are you?" and the smile travelled from lips to eyes.

Memories of Maurice being asked the same question came to Liadan and she smiled; he had loved flirting with Sylvia, giving her a sly hug, enjoying her liking for him.

"Warm, a chara," he would answer "very warm."

Maurice may have felt warm with Sylvia, but Felicity and Liadan did not and Sylvia resented this. Sylvia, however, felt that they should have been friends. Maurice appreciated her warm, welcoming air, her intense interest in everything he said and her touch upon his shoulder. Sylvia was a modern woman: she wore her clothes with style; her hair was saloon perfect; she did her shopping where the "Television Weather Girls" shopped. Felicity would have recognised the stylist cut, but that they had so much in common, Sylvia would never be allowed to know. The gossip between Sylvia and Tom would not have helped.

"How's your Dad?" She smiled sweetly at Ronan.

"How's Felicity?" Sylvia asked less sweetly "I haven't seen her in ages."

"Away in Norway skiing," Liadan explained, "At least right now she is skiing, later she will be working."

"Skiing and at her age - isn't she great!"

Liadan knew instinctively not to react. Felicity was certainly not old and probably about five years younger than Sylvia, but Sylvia wanted to snipe; to protest would have been useless. Sylvia would have insisted that Felicity did not look her age. Liadan had played this game with Sylvia before.

"She'll be back soon; we are hoping to get away again at Easter. Have you any plans yourself."

"Some people have to work," Sylvia said with a grimace.

The wooden door of the café scraped as another customer entered. The kitchen chairs clattered on the stone flags. The smell of roasting coffee circulated in the room again with the new infusion of fresh clean air. Liadan looked quickly around the large gloomy space. Most tables were already filled. Having exchanged greetings and enquired sufficiently, Liadan felt she could, with complete propriety, order and take a table.

"Two large cups of coffee please and a couple of pastries... we've been working hard," she said. She was not going to let Sylvia have it all her own way. Sylvia's head had tipped to one side and Liadan felt under pressure to point out that indeed they had been working: a lot of letter writing, doing donkey work, producing notices of exclusion, worthless bits of paper perhaps, but they had produced them endlessly. Most importantly they had written to Jane Fitzwilliam that afternoon, she thought.

Of course this would not be work to Sylvia, who had on a previous occasion been heard to remark:

"Behaving like a student protesting and such, no manners, hanging around, drinking coffee, t-shirts in this sort of weather. If she was my daughter..." and the rest would be left to head shaking.

Not remembering to thank Sylvia when the coffee pot and cups were placed on the counter did not increase any ideas of good opinion and Sylvia turned to her next customer with a sweet smile on her face and a little nod of connivance - the lack of manners in that young one!

Ronan found a corner table as far as possible away from the counter - a dark little spot - and although one seat was occupied already by the time Liadan arrived, the occupant had left it.

"He'll be back." Ronan warned before disappearing towards the men's room.   Liadan sat down hardly noticing what he said. The files placed precariously on the table beside her elbow occupied all her attention as they wobbled towards the edge; she sipped her coffee and ate the pastry. By the time the man returned Liadan had completely forgotten about him and had moved into his place. He stood in the shadows, his head above the low lights on the table; although she did not see him she felt him hovering over her and she got up. Her reaction to his arrival had been so slow that, when she stood up, he had turned away. She moved further along the table, making way for him. When he turned around he had wound a thick scarf over his mouth and nose and turned up the black collar of his coat over his neck and ears. The only part of his face visible was unfriendly eyes. They seemed like dark pits in the grey sludge of poor lighting. He made her feel uncomfortable and she fingered the half-eaten pastry.

"I'm sorry, I thought you'd gone," she said grudgingly as she leant forward, sweeping the crumbs over to her side of the table.

He answered, " Don't let me interfere with your enjoyment. Help yourself, please do." His accent was mid-Atlantic, mixed with a touch of something very foreign. She detected chill and sarcasm in his voice. If he had not been so cold and brusque she would not have snapped back.

"Why not? Who do you think you are?"

 She had moved herself completely out of his space and now she decided to ignore him. She had apologised; what more did he want? As Ronan came towards them, the man, who had not sat down, knocked the table with his foot as he left, spilling her coffee and disturbing her files. Liadan jumped to her feet.

"What a twerp!" But he had gone.

"What a horrible man! He should crawl back into a hole," she cried to Ronan, mopping the coffee spills. They both laughed.

"I said I was sorry." Liadan sat down, still aggrieved, "A total moron. I know he kicked the table on purpose."

There was something uncomfortable about the incident with the man and they both fell silent.

They finished their coffee. Liadan took her coat from the back of her chair, catching the table with her foot. The clattering and banging turned everyone's attention to her and, as she reached inside her coat pocket for her keys, Sylvia appeared.

"You left your pastries on the counter," she said, before moving on.

In a flash the whole horrid scene became clear: she had placed her files on the tray beside her coffee; she had placed some further folders under her arm and then she had struggled to reach the distant, free table; she had presumed that Ronan had collected the pastries, and she had eaten the pastry left on the table: his pastry.

In a flash she saw his face - his cold, staring eyes. "Oh for goodness sake," she thought. She felt bothered by the whole thing and did not see any humour in it.

Ronan laughed. "Come on, it's only a pastry."

"He looked poor," she said

"Unkempt, more like."

Liadan sat down – yes, he looked familiar. "Oh my God! Was it Paddy?"

If she rushed she would probably catch him, explain what happened, but she did not move; she felt rejection. No, he had not recognised her, but somehow she felt it would not have made any difference.

"Oh, for goodness sake," she said, irritated with herself.

"Possession is nine tenths of the law..." Ronan laughed, "Where's his sense of humour?"

But Liadan's sense of humour had also disappeared. She felt this relatively insignificant occurrence intensely: it was like a physical force, unjust, unwarranted, a violence to her system. It was a moment of magnitude and created a space into which she felt she was being sucked, where everything was again thrown into terrible confusion. Paddy was the only living person who had been present that day: he was the only one who knew what she now knew. His were the arms into which she had always believed she could run, like the little girl of former years, for comfort and understanding. She had been waiting for his return with such longing, thinking that it would also, to some small degree, be the return of those others who were gone. She would be able to share with him, as with no other, the memories of those times. The presence of Ronan now irritated her: he seemed like an intruder and his sympathy was out of place, inappropriate and incompatible with her present emotions.

Fifteen minutes later they left the café. Liadan hung her head; she begged the Fates to allow her to make her way home without having to see Paddy.

He had come back, as Wendy said he would.

* * *

Their first meeting had been a disaster and the telling of it had only aggravated her feelings of unhappiness and despair: if Liadan had told the story herself of how they had met again after so many years, she would have made light of the incident - the mistake had been hers after all. Instead she heard that Paddy had told Wendy about their meeting. He had not recognised her because she had turned into such a spoilt little madam. His meaning maybe, not his actual words, for Liadan suspected Wendy did not quote verbatim.

"He said he hadn't noticed you coming in, and the next thing he knew you were taking over the table, putting your files everywhere. He had nowhere to sit." Wendy giggled a little.

"No! That's not true; there was nobody at the table. Oh! What's the difference?"

Was there just a touch of pleasure in Wendy's voice? Liadan forced her lips to smile, but her heart hurt. "It wasn't that bad," she protested. She felt helpless and inadequate; she realised that she was merely exposing her fragility to an unsympathetic audience.

"He's changed and you've changed; it's no wonder he didn't recognise you." They both walked in silence. "We met up at Joe's." Wendy answered Liadan's questioning look. It was easy to see that Liadan wanted to know more but was too proud to ask.

"He's not seeing many people at the moment," she went on.

"*People*...well I won't be inviting him around anyway," Liadan said close to tears.

"I didn't mean..."

"What didn't you mean?"

"I didn't mean...oh nothing." Wendy also seemed to feel that there was no point in continuing. Liadan and she had never been close. The present circumstances and the aggravated atmosphere were not likely to lead to confidences. Wendy liked facility and here there certainly would be none.

CHAPTER 16

"Lucy, sometimes I just wonder." Liadan was sitting on the hood of the Aga cooker, her feet on a kitchen chair.

"Never mind them, love," Lucy replied and from years of practice she went on reading her book without losing track or missing a word of Liadan's moaning.

"Wendy's no help at all: she says Pastures New is sold and that Paddy told her he wanted it sold. There's nothing now that can be done."

"Is that a fact indeed? What happened to her? Haven't seen her for ages. Did I tell you Tinker had some kittens in the cowshed?"

"She's always with Paddy..."

Lucy closed her book.

"Never mind..."

"I don't mind, I'm just telling you." Liadan snapped.

Lucy looked in an unsettled way at Liadan: she knew what she was being told, but she had no adequate response to give. Liadan glowed in her heart like the burnish on the copper saucepans that lined the walls. Lucy could find her way in the vagaries of a young heart, and most particularly in those of this young heart, much more accurately than others who had more direct experience of the wayfaring of young affections, and she knew that a certain reticence, a certain reserve would relieve and assist where interference and intrusion would simply lay waste, and so she kept silent.

***

When Paddy and Liadan met again it was by the lake. This time she recognised him immediately: he was on her territory. She had gone to the lake to swim, her first swim for a long time. Previous days had been warm but that morning frost had lain visible in dark places and by late afternoon the sky was grey-blue, a weak sun skimming the earth like a stone on a pond. Each year these first swims of the season were very hard to get going, but she had to quieten herself and be a part of the lake again. While she swam quickly far into the northern waters, faint splashes and shadows were the only intruders. It seemed a natural form of therapy and its harshness helped her to escape her feeling of loss, a feeling which now had reached almost suffocating proportions: the Fitzwilliams had signed the contract; the house was sold. No explanations had been given to Liadan and she felt devastated, but also mystified. Could it be true that Jane Fitzwilliam wanted her husband's body found? With Maurice dead for three years now, revenge could not be a motive.

Liadan swam to the bank. Paddy stood there watching her with the same stooped intensity she remembered from all those years ago when he had looked down on her as she lay on the ground after her fall. Less the vagrant, just a strange person, a mix of the old Paddy – strong and good looking, and the new - stern and critical. He did not try to look away when Liadan's eyes met his and his eyes were still on her as she struggled to reach her towel. He even walked along the bank towards her. As he neared, she thought she could detect something else in his eyes, something malevolent. For a moment she wondered if she should scream; it seemed too ridiculous - he was, after all, Paddy. Instead she said rudely, trying to hide the uneasiness she felt:

"Back off, can't you?"

She scrambled from the lake, finding the rough brick steps Maurice had put in below the boathouse.

"Did I frighten you?" He did not back off.

"No, not exactly," she answered feeling foolish, and yet … "Why are you creeping around?" She tried to laugh. She clutched the towel to her, and glancing towards him she saw that he was not taken in by her attempted light-heartedness. His face seemed set in a mixture of dislike, vindictiveness and rancour. Feeling the intensity of his hostility she snapped:

"I just didn't expect anyone, that's all."

"Well... we must respect your privacy," he answered and, although he did smile in a wry sort of way, she could not bring herself to respond lightly. It was all wrong: she really did not want to be rude to Paddy, but he frightened her and made her feel vulnerable. A little empathy, a little understanding could not be so difficult. Could he not make any allowances? She felt bad about what happened at the Café. She had expected to be hugging him, to be telling him about the awfulness of the years since he had left; listening to all he had gone through, but most of all Liadan had expected to talk about Anna with him: nobody else would do. She had looked forward to being able to talk about their loss, about the times that they had shared and that only they could understand. As they stood facing each other the silence grew like mould between them, preventing the catharsis that she had longed for.

She dried her chin again and again. Very soon she would start to shiver and the very thought that she would look so weak filled her with anger. She had made up her mind to tell him to go when he said:

"I've heard the road is going through here and I wanted to see the lake again." A very long pause ensued and then he said. "It's an anxious time for me... I believe you received a letter from your father explaining what happened?" He spoke hastily: it was as if he were saying what he had to say as quickly as he could - getting it over with.

"I suppose Wendy told you?" Liadan said tightly.

So presumptuous of Wendy to tell him anything! Now he expected her to divulge what was so much her own private business, while at the same time, expecting her to put up with his unfriendly behaviour. Through this sale that apparently he wished to go ahead with, his mother and her greed were now exposing them all, and this was bad enough, but how could he stand there and turn his back on Anna's memory? The memory of her whose image stood before them? This she would never allow.

"I'm surprised you have the guts to come here." The moment the words were spoken she regretted them. The same look that she had seen in the café swept over his face.

"Well...I mean..." she hesitated, but then rushed on "I would've thought you'd want to forget... my father told me everything." She spoke in haste and with growing despair, longing to unsay what she had said. She looked away. Sometimes she even had the feeling that maybe she did not know everything. How did he manage to put her in the wrong? Her father's letter locked away in her writing desk had told her only his side of events. Maybe... and as she looked troubled and uncertain he seemed to read her thoughts:

"I don't believe he told you... What have they told you, I wonder? ...all of them pretending..." He shook his head; his face looked grim. "Anyway my mother wanted...to be honest she didn't want him found while she was alive, but now there is no reason to delay selling up just for your convenience."

"OUR CONVENIENCE!" Liadan shouted; sometimes the only valid form of defence was attack and so she chose it:

"I remember a lot of what happened and I keep remembering more... I'd be worried if I were you." Her threat was as vague as her memory.

"Did your father tell you why? No...I didn't think so," he snapped ignoring her threat.

The lake sighed behind them, or seemed to, with the gentle movement of tiny waves against the steps. It should have drawn them back into the past, helped them to clear the turmoil between them. But its only power now was to divide them:

"No!" he said again concluding that her silence was a sign of concurrence. His face twitched and a momentary look of pity told her what he thought of her family. He knew what had happened. He knew the truth. She felt rage welling up inside her. Bending down she tugged at her trainers and stumbled. Did he look away just then or would he have liked to see her fall backwards into the lake? His helping hand came too late when it was offered. She managed to right herself and with no lack of intention she flicked his face with her wet towel as she spun it around over her shoulders. Then she in her turn looked away, pretending not to have seen what she had done. Over her wet clothes she pulled her fleece. The deep hood hid her face in its thick brown wool. When she turned again nothing in his demeanour showed that she had hurt him and yet a red mark had appeared just below his eyes. Both of them stood looking over the gloomy, green water. Neither sound nor stir was heard by them, as their surroundings seemed to step back away from the conflict. An intense feeling of being on a different plane, standing still with the world racing backwards to the time when everything had happened, threw the present moment into a nonsensical turmoil.

As Liadan often found now when trying to interact with people, her emotion got the better of her. She floundered around like a fish on dry land. She felt a huge bitterness against certain people and she knew that she would not forgive any of them, ever. Out of this whole long history, at a very young age, she had inherited an enormous burden of uncertainty and guilt. She was completely alone in her search for those who were culpable; her search was a partial one because the idea that those she had loved were guilty and now dead was one that she was completely unable to countenance.

The cold became unbearable and she began to shiver. She wanted to get away from him and go back up to the house, to reach the security of her room, to throw the towel down on her bed, open her letter, hold it to her to feel the comfort of her father's writing while the lake's sweet scent invaded her room. Let this meeting happen sometime in the future, somewhere else where there were other people. She felt too vulnerable here alone with him. They could meet somewhere; they could sit and confront each other. It was obvious now that their contact would be one that she had never imagined; she would have to find her way in the labyrinth of a personality that she found she knew nothing about. The person that stood between her and the sanctuary of the house and her room was a stranger: he stood in her way and the words were not there to ask him to move. From where she stood the house seemed so many miles away.

"The road will come willy-nilly. It's not my responsibility to explain the rest. I suggest you ask your *step*-mother. It will in the end become plain what really happened. For my mother's sake I have said nothing before. I hope your father kept his side of the bargain - though it's not important to me." He shrugged his shoulders; he did not care. "I'm not going to expose anything, as I promised her, but I'm not going to try to stop it coming to light ... so talk to your stepmother; she'll know."

What would Felicity know? He revolted her with his inappropriate talk. Up and down, forward and back her emotions rolled and he kept pushing. She wanted to contradict him. To show how strong she was.

"I really don't know what you're talking about. The road is coming... thanks to your mother," she pointed out; her realisation of what was implicit in his account was very fragmentary. "I don't know anything about any bargain. Your mother shouldn't have sold." She made a motion with her hand, pushing him away. "I want to get dressed."

"Look, if you'd stop thinking of yourself all the time you would have realised by now – my mother is dead."

Liadan's face became stony; she whispered "I'm sorry." It seemed as though the whole horrible situation had dug itself into a deep cavern of nobody's making and yet somebody must be to blame, but who? She had not known; she had not known so many things. Perhaps he was right and she should also feel accountable. But why? She had been just a child and had tried so desperately to remember, but at the same time to forget.

He turned his back on her and continued to talk. "I sold up..." and then shrugging impatiently - "Dress by all means; nobody is going to molest you. You do know, Liadan, that morally you should show your letter if my father's body is found; that was what was understood between my mother and your father. He promised her that, in return for her silence, he would write a letter to you explaining his part in my father's death and my innocence: that was the deal," Paddy insisted. For myself I don't really care, but for my mother's reputation…," he started to move away but Liadan could not let him go like this; she needed to know so much more. It was too horrible that the tortured hours that her father had spent trying to compose in anguished and confused distress had been spent, not in an effort to reassure and protect her, but because he was under some obligation, some coercion to tell something that in the end he had not told.

"Then why did you come back?" she asked, before she could stop herself. "Why? Why did you sell? We could have kept the shelter secret."

"I thought it was clear to you that my mother lost everything because of your family. Now that there is a good chance my father's body will be found, I have come to see that no one tries to dirty her name. I will see that things are made clear, that everybody knows: posthumous justice, that's what I want. What took place here ruined her life. Yes, I have sold the farm. I want to start afresh. The farm was mine." A dryness or change of tension in his throat made his voice less harsh.

"I didn't know," Liadan mumbled, "I really didn't know… I'm sorry…"

"No more hiding! She shouldn't have suffered!" he cut in, not listening to her.

But again he had snubbed her: Liadan listened in disbelief. All this bitterness should have been hers. He talked of himself and his, and the things that he said were wrong. His mother had died, but so had her father; so had Anna. She did not want him near her any more. Not once had he spoken of Anna. If he had cried Liadan would have understood. Anguish and tears for Anna were what she had expected. She had imagined how their first meeting would be: they would fall into each others arms, be comforted at last. Was he suffering from amnesia?

"I understand why you want things to remain hidden." She heard contempt in his voice.

"You should have wanted the same thing," she replied, her voice breaking.

"This lake will be drained and maybe you'll be the wiser. I would happily tell you, but I promised my mother..."

"So you keep saying," she said. She was dressed now and she felt more relaxed. She knew that he was taunting her, trying to get her to ask, but she would not ask. She looked around her and felt the scenes of the past returning, gently at first and then in a huge surge, so that she could almost hear the voices of those long and happy summers filling the air. "There's nothing here for you...nothing! This is Anna's lake," she whispered suddenly exhausted; "How?" she whispered, "but how?"... the question remained unformulated: the anguish was too great.

"Oh Anna, our dear, departed Anna." His words were bile-laden and Liadan caught her breath. And then he said, "Anna... oh Anna," his voice had turned to grief and she could hardly bear to hear it: "I won't be back."

He walked down the path away from the house. He walked past the shelter and then on and out of her view. His figure seemed to blend gradually into the trees and although she watched, she could not see him reappearing on the other side of the lake, on the grassy bank where she had given her bucket of eels to that same Paddy all those years ago. Shocked and trembling, she stood cowed and isolated on the bank. A feeling of desolation overwhelmed her. She wanted to cry out so that he might hear her. But there was no point: she knew he would be pitiless. How could he have spoken of Anna in that way? As though... she could not bear to think... as if... he were talking about someone who was utterly worthless?

"I hate him..." she wanted to scream. She felt more alone now than she had for a long time; it was like a sudden bereavement. In her mind Paddy had been a friend; she had talked to him endlessly even though he had been so far away, even though sometimes she had thought that he might also be dead. This new Paddy she feared; he did not love her, he did not love anybody belonging to her. It must have always been like that and she had been too young and had not known.

The daylight was finished. Evening time had arrived quickly and darkness came down suddenly. She could hear the yard bell tolling; in years gone by it would have summoned her father from a distant field. Now it continued to warn the men who worked on the farm that the cows were coming home and that they must come in from where they were out in the fields to milk them; they would come gladly towards this daily appointment, the final one of the working day; laughing and talking, they would herd the cows into the sheds, attach the machines, milk them and then release them for the night. Very shortly too the road excavators would fall silent; their gradual crawl brought them inexorably nearer each day. Today they were poised at Garrvine Hill. Soon they would appear coming around towards the north of the lake.

Now the silence of the countryside was regained and complete. Only the shuffling and wing flutter of birds settling and the faint sound of mice in the brambles was a reminder of life continuing on, unaffected by the darkness which for her filled this moment. She gathered up the rest of her clothes and pulled her fleece more tightly. She had a feeling he might be there in the dusk, and she shivered with disquiet.

***

Liadan sat alone in the Cotton Tree Cafe waiting for Ronan. She was deep in thought as she slowly ate the hot broccoli soup. Sylvia stood at the table questioning and Liadan wished she would go away.

"They say she had cancer you know... Is it true?" Sylvia asked. Liadan wondered who Sylvia was talking about, but as Gerry Moore moved near the table, sniffing the air like a bloodhound, Sylvia switched her attention to him.

"It's really tasty," Liadan confirmed looking up, but he moved quickly away, responding to a sharp female voice.

Sylvia smirked. "Oh dear! How long will this one last?" she asked, not expecting any particular answer. "She's a city lass! City lass meets pig farmer...maybe not."

Liadan thought of Ronan and a smile touched her lips. Handsome, clever lawyer meets interested country girl? Decidedly yes! In a funny sort of way she had Paddy to thank for their closeness. It had been Ronan she had run to after the meeting at the lake. He had reacted in a sure and yet restrained way; he had not shown any signs of wanting to dismiss or belittle; he had not underestimated what she was suffering. With consideration he had gently managed to brush aside the childlike longing she had harboured for Paddy. She had finally lost all sense of herself as she clung to him tightly that first night, losing herself in her desire for him. She loved him entirely. She could not keep her eyes off him. He had been her best friend. He accepted everything about her. He was tolerant and understanding and sometimes the way he lay by her side reminded her of Anna's attentiveness. Unexpectedly she had found that he had filled the void and she did not feel alone any more.

When Paddy and Wendy entered the café Liadan felt that unfailing surge of hurt and betrayal, but now it was bearable. The two were so engrossed in each other that they were standing by Liadan's table before either noticed her. Wendy gasped and gushed a bit before moving further on to where Paddy stood holding a chair in readiness.

"Let's meet up," she called.

Ronan appeared just then and his soup followed closely behind in Sylvia's hands.

"Lung cancer I heard," Sylvia said again. "You're Wendy's friend ... didn't she tell you. No one seems to know for sure."

"Wendy..." A look of horror swept Liadan's face.

"Of course not." Sylvia shrugged her shoulders; Liadan was always so unaware. "Jane Fitzwilliam, didn't you know? She's dead; that's why he's back."

"Everyone thinks they know why he's back," Liadan thought.

Ronan took her hand. And she could see from his face:

"You knew?" she asked, with a shadow of annoyance clouding her face.

"About Jane? Only recently." A look of guilt momentarily crossed his face. "I didn't tell you before because I couldn't, she was our client...*I couldn't*...Lia ...sorry...only knew recently, honest," he murmured quickly.

"Oh it doesn't matter. Paddy told me at the lake – it's just that everyone seems to have known for ages and ages. I wish I had, then maybe I could have handled things better... couldn't you just have told me?" she asked.

"Now Lia...I couldn't...you know."

The town girl and pig farmer at the next table raised their voices in anger, interrupting Ronan's admonishment.

"You told me you'd finish with her." The girlfriend's voice flared up. "I believed you. No! You're not the man I thought you were."

"Hush dear!" murmured Gerry's much lower voice, " Don't want the world to know our business."

"I don't care who hears," came the reply but in a much lower voice.

"Ah sweetheart. It'd be a criminal waste of good wool." Gerry's voice pleaded.

Every ear in the room turned towards the red-faced Gerry.

"What are they on about?" Ronan asked.

Sylvia came by again smirking. "The old girlfriend was knitting a jumper for him ... I expect he's waiting for her to finish it."

Laughing Ronan whispered, "No more secrets for us. It's a deal. We'll always trust each other, won't we Lia?"

Liadan felt her heart pounding. What could she honestly say? She had a massive secret. How could she tell Ronan? She loved him, but he was a lawyer and the lawyer of a family whose interests were opposed to her own. How could she say to him: "Guess where Tom Fitzwilliam is buried!" or even, "Daddy didn't mean to hurt him, but he buried him in the shelter. We have to keep it a secret." Ronan was too honest, too straightforward, and he would insist on telling the police. She knew this.

* * *

The day before the body was found, Liadan, Paddy and Wendy met again on a narrow lane that divided Tuskar Rock House

estate from the land belonging to Pastures New. Liadan saw
Paddy and Wendy at some distance striding towards her, hand
in hand and she knew that unless she retraced her steps, they
would have to meet. The hedge on either side of her grew tall
and thick, shielding the lane from the drying sun, leaving large
water-filled potholes that, for all of them, required attention to
their footing. Now and then the spring sun did break through
to glisten on the early lime-green blades of grass, bent double
by fresh rainwater. In between the grasses, cobblestones from
an ancient road were visible among dark-brown, rotting leaves
heaved over by earthworms. As she walked forward Liadan
lifted her head to see them advance in her direction and a million greetings ran through her mind. They must see her, she
thought, yet still they strode on towards her: perhaps they intended to walk by without salutation. Within a second or two
she and they would be in touching distance of each other and,
just as Liadan thought of this, they stopped, as if they had only
then spotted her. They seemed so put-out that Liadan forgot all
her friendly greetings and said:

"I am perfectly entitled to be here, you know."

"Liadan!" Wendy and Paddy said at the same time and
looked at each other in amazement. "Of course you are entitled
to be here." Wendy said with warmth in her voice. "We're so
pleased to see you, aren't we Paddy? It will give Paddy an opportunity to talk about what happened at the lake. He wants to
start again."

Liadan blushed and stammered. "Well?"

"I understand how alarming it must have been for you. I
should have asked your permission to be there."

"Please go there any time you wish" she said stiffly " I don't
go there any more; most of the area is ruined by the road."

"Yes, it has to be faced," he said.

"Well you're not going to get me to agree to that." Liadan
said, smiling wryly and he immediately moved on, being forced
by the deep potholes to pass so close to her that she caught
her breath. Wendy followed him, but moved away closer to the
hedge.

"Oh!" Wendy said "Maybe it's for the best."

"For whose best?" Liadan asked.

Wendy shrugged her shoulders. "I'm sorry. Really I am, Liadan."

But Liadan could only feel dislike for her.

"Liadan, please…" Wendy tried again. "Paddy told me and I know he's sorry," she said at last.

"At last an apology from Mr Fitzwilliam or rather from his agent, even though a little too late and second-hand." Liadan could not stop herself and she watched with some unease as Paddy strode back towards her. He laughed in a funny way. Wendy caught his arm and whispered, "Don't! Remember you promised."

"I don't blame you of course," he said.

"Don't!" Wendy said again. "It's not her fault."

Liadan trembled a little; he turned to Wendy, "I know, but she has to know."

"No!" Wendy tugged his arm.

"I was forced away all those years ago." Bitterness filled the air, "I have never been able to speak out about what really happened and now I am still being held back." He spoke vehemently, frightening Liadan and so she attacked:

"How dare you. Is something missing or don't you remember?" she screamed "You're alive. What about Anna?"

She could hardly hear him for the loud throbbing in her ears. "Anna was the reason it all happened," he whispered, and then his voice went so soft it was as though a breeze spoke his words. "I am sorry for what happened to Anna. You know I loved her. When I went away, every moment of every day I mourned. I hope that no such desolation is ever your lot. She was my soul; I loved her unstintingly to the day she died – even though I knew all. But when she died that love changed. I can never, ever forgive her."

Wendy pulled at him and succeeded in propelling him away.

Left alone Liadan stood watching them become smaller as they strode down the lane, and she stood continuing to watch the lane when they had disappeared from view.

"Felicity's right: the man's deranged," she thought, and then she thought with more understanding: "It's true what Lucy said: Anna's death drove him mad."

CHAPTER 17

1984

"I wondered if you would come," Liadan said to Superintendent Furlong at the hall door.

"I thought I'd have a word!" Superintendent Furlong seemed in agreement with her wondering. "I thought I'd better call just to keep you in the picture; you're bound to be curious and I spotted you on the balcony the other day when we removed the body. The remains are with the coroner and our investigations have started." Harry Furlong grunted a bit.

He was somewhat uneasy. He felt a little out of his element, a little at sea. She was young and pretty, obviously carefully brought up and, because of her age, could not possibly be involved in this business of the body; but then again, she could know something; she might be hiding something. He would, all the same, have to talk to her.

Liadan was a bit defensive. "It was on our land, after all." He gave her a look as much as to say "Not any more."

Liadan thought she might be starting to "go off" the superintendent just a little and she thought to herself that she would put Lucy straight about him. Lucy had said Harry Furlong was not too smart to talk to ordinary souls, but Liadan was beginning to wonder at least about the "smartness" side of things.

"As it is a murder enquiry I …" The superintendent started.

"Murder? No!" Liadan changed from cool young lady to crazed adolescent. "No, no!" she stormed. "We heard you'd arrested Paddy. *I couldn't believe it….* How can you be so stupid?"

Superintendent Furlong flinched. "Young lady, that's no way to speak to me. You're young enough to be my daughter. You should have some respect…"

"But…" Liadan's face seemed to howl in exasperation and Harry Furlong relented. "Oh, I haven't arrested Mr Fitzwilliam; he came to see me of his own accord. He'd heard... the whole world seems to have heard."

A bleak March sunset sent shadows of the house chasing down the gravel sweep, leaving a chill swathe of air behind. Bright narcissi nearby glimmered in the hall-door light, further away the white faces of the flowers disappeared into the obscurity of the long grass. To Liadan it felt as though they were going to stand there forever. She wondered if she ought to apologise; she knew she should have asked him in, but she just stood there hesitating.

"What nonsense! I haven't arrested the young man," the superintendent grumbled again.

"It's Tom Fitzwilliam, Paddy's father. It was an accident," she said, and her hand dashed all over her face as though fending off imaginary flying objects.

"Well now, so Mr Fitzwilliam said. Dental records will confirm all of this, but there's no reason not to believe it's him. I'm certainly interested in what you have to say, and do wonder how you know. But let's go in- *somewhere warmer*! I need to speak to your mother... I mean stepmother," he quickly corrected himself.

Liadan nodded and stepped back through the stone-arched doorway and Harry's voice boomed into the empty hall.

"I'm sorry to say that it is a murder case. A bullet was found lodged in the skeleton's backbone and that makes it a serious business."

This was simply not possible: Liadan knew it could not be. Her father had expended so much time and energy; he had so sincerely suffered. She had watched those dreadful days towards the end of his life when, even though at the time she had been dismissive and often sarcastic with him, she had known that he was trying to communicate, to tell her... He had written the letter; he had told the truth. He could not possibly have done otherwise. Now she was stopped in her tracks:

"No, there wasn't a bullet, really there wasn't." She was panicked; her thinking became confused. Away went the certainty of a moment ago. Her father's letter had not mentioned anything like that: "*Oh Daddy,*" she thought, "you promised to tell me the truth." Her mouth twisted in alarm and she pressed her fingers into her scalp. "He wrote a letter saying what happened, you know. He said it was an accident. I don't expect that you would consider that my father would lie about something that was so important. He was there, you know; he would not have lied to me."

"Let's speak to Mrs Agan," the superintendent said smoothly. "We'd like to have a bit of a chat with you and Mrs Agan. It's only the beginning - no need to worry, my dear. Any help you can give us will be very welcome indeed."

"But I don't see how I can be of any help." Her head felt tight and her breath was uneven.

"We'd like to see what your father wrote," the superintendent replied.

"Well you can't," Liadan answered quickly and uncertainly, but with a definite sharpness.

Liadan could feel the superintendent's eyes on her back. She walked ahead carefully, avoiding cracks in the marble floor; at every second footstep she touched the panelling along the wall of the hall. She turned when she reached the staircase and the stand where a statue of Mercury stood. The inspector's soft and lumbering gait was heard only as a soft, padding echo in the emptiness of the marble hall.

"We'll get to the truth, don't you worry," Harry Furlong said to no one in particular. A cliché here or there usually calmed fraught encounters, but Liadan took offence.

"Good God!" she swore.

"And so say all of us," Harry retorted cheerfully, but when Liadan stared hard at him, he looked back with a hurt look on his face.

"I meant…." She hesitated.

"Exactly."

The whole business was going badly: "Why was it so tricky?" Liadan wondered. Perhaps she would tell him; not bits here and there, but all that she could remember, all that she had read in the letter. Showing the letter was now out of the question. Until she knew what really happened she would not surrender the letter. Supposing her father had lied to her, the shame would be unbearable. She needed help; she needed to get a grip. Jumping out of her skin and straight down his throat would not help.

Opening a door near the back of the staircase they stepped into a small, stone, windowless corridor where their footsteps continued to echo. The sweet smell of a wood-burning stove wafted up to them and there were low-lying, dusky traces of smoke along the edges of the corridor.

Liadan beckoned to him; there was no longer a need to step over cracks or joins. The colder air of the corridor made the superintendent sneeze and while fumbling in his pocket for a handkerchief he counted the rows of antique, coiled, metal bells high above their heads. According to the display of bells on the wall, the house had fifteen bedrooms and probably more.

"Most of the house is closed up; we're moving out," Liadan explained "and we're living in my father's old work rooms. Felicity is around somewhere."

They came to an oak door with a chipped porcelain key plate; the handle rattled loosely in the door; Liadan leant her shoulder against it pushing it open and immediately an inferno of heat and light lit their cold faces. The small room, unlike the great empty rooms they had quickly passed by, looked crowded. A woman knelt by the fire throwing wads of paper into the flame, each one picked from a ready stack by her side. On the mantelpiece a higgledy-piggledy array of books, lamps and pictures were balanced, some more precariously than others. Glass-fronted bookcases on either side of the chimney breast contained an equally eclectic collection. There were overturned armchairs near the back of the room and a large green desk with unevenly opened drawers. Nearer the door, stacked on the floor, were filing boxes and Liadan and the Inspector climbed over these boxes, eagerly approaching the fire.

"My step-mother, Felicity – Superintendent Furlong," Liadan said as Felicity pulled herself up with the help of the mantelpiece.

"*Do* come in… sit down, *won't you*…wherever you can," she said and the superintendent obeyed dropping heavily on to the sofa, making the cushions bounce and stretching his hands towards the blaze.

"I was hoping to see you Mrs Agan, and hope it is not at too inconvenient a time. I expect you know we…." the Superintendent said, and hesitating he added, "I believe we're looking at a murder enquiry." He was finally matter-of-fact and there was very little regret in his voice.

"Yes, a murder enquiry," he repeated.

With one rigid finger Liadan stabbed the sofa arm.

"That's rubbish," she said.

"Indeed!" Mrs Agan interrupted her stepdaughter's outburst, "murder…*surely* not, superintendent… but of course we will do our very best to assist you. Won't we, Darling? Do go to the kitchen and see if Lucy will bring us in some tea." she continued, addressing Liadan.

"Liadan …I believe you wanted to show us your father's letter?" the superintendent said quickly fearing that control might fall to the very composed lady, who had drawn herself up and seated herself quietly in an armchair.

A feeling of helplessness came over Liadan. If she showed the letter it would not assist Paddy; not that she much wanted to any more, but it had been her father's wish; perhaps this was because it might make matters worse for the Fitzwilliams? She was not sure of anything anymore. Her eyes roamed about the room and instead of stabbing at the arm of the sofa, she kneaded it like dough. She looked at Felicity, willing her into action. If only she could think, but nothing seemed to come to her except a whirling feeling in her head. Paddy would blame her; he would never speak to her again and she had to help him for Anna's sake. Then voices intruded on her muddled mind.

"We're moving *on* you know, getting rid of old memories. We didn't want to *keep* looking back." Felicity moved forward with her poker. She thumped the logs making them collapse and the papers nestling above lit up. Letters and notes, invoices and diaries, a bundle of old papers scorched and curled as they burned, lighting the kindling beneath, with sparks exploding into the room. "Getting rid of old memories; I think you've come too late Superintendent."

"Maurice Agan's letter?" the Inspector almost beseeched.

"Liadan?" Superintendent Furlong's voice lowered an octave, "about your father's letter?"

"I don't know...I haven't got it any more," Liadan stammered.

"*Everything is gone* – letters and all other unofficial documents... only this morning. We couldn't take all that with us, you know. Would you like that tea now?" Felicity smiled as if nothing were amiss. She lifted the poker driving it into the logs; everything, above and below, was united in a burst of flame.

Chapter 18

1984

"Have they got the report yet?" Harry Furlong asked, as he pushed into the lobby. He pulled his heavy black coat from his shoulder. He had a headache; he felt feverish and because of this, his impatience about the date for the inquest was more acute.

"You'll be the first... if I get anything. I'll bring it up myself."

"They know I'm in a hurry, I hope?" Harry asked as he made his way to the stairs.

"Hurry-up Harry," the sergeant said under his breath.

Harry knew the sergeant would be a bit anxious that he might have heard:

"What was that?" he growled. 'Hurry up' was his nickname - he quite liked it really. He was not without a sense of humour: he liked being a presence, being a manifestation of something, and why not of impatience. The somewhat irreverent attention that he received from his sergeant was a good deal better than being disregarded.

Restraining a cough that might otherwise tear at his sore windpipe, he climbed the stairs, two at a time. He sat down at his desk having decided to put his coat back on. With the *post mortem* now over and the coroner's phone call to tell him that the skeleton showed signs of general trauma - a broken rib maybe two, one prior to death, the other not so clear, a fractured eye socket and a nasty bullet lodged in the coccyx, or words to that effect - Harry felt that he had what he needed: the report would be nice when it came, but the date for the inquest would be even better. Everything seemed to suggest that the skeleton was Tom Fitzwilliam's; all that was needed now was a report attributing the correct age and describing a full set of teeth and the question of identity would be closed.

"Merciful heaven!" Harry muttered to himself, "What a beating that poor fellow got." Just as well his wife was dead; there was only Paddy, his son, left to mourn him. Paddy had made it clear that for him the story was closed and he had insisted that the whole thing had been an accident. They had fought all three of them, Maurice, Paddy and Tom and Tom had died, or so Paddy had claimed. Of course the Inspector did not believe him, but he did find it very strange how detached the young man seemed. Even supposing he was telling the truth, his lack of emotion with regard to his father's death would suggest that "the accident" was not an unwelcome one. And yet he looked so worn and thin for such a young man. Certainly if he was not suffering now, he must have in the past.

Harry held his breath: poor Mrs Fitzwilliam. It was hard to imagine how dreadful it would have been if she had known that her husband had been beaten up and then shot and was lying not far from her house, but...she must have known something. How did they buy her silence? And he had a bit of a reputation; Harry had almost forgotten. Best not to jump to conclusions. His head sunk between his shoulders as though it were weighed down by his thoughts. He must make sure that Jane Fitzwilliam had really died of whatever it was, last year. "Dear me, all this paperwork." In the end he would be forced to have someone in full time to go through it all: sifting and discarding, arranging and filing. He did not like the idea: he knew, in all the dreadful disorder that surrounded him, where everything was and, anyway, who would know what to keep and what to discard?

Harry lifted his phone to speak to the duty sergeant. "Get Paddy Fitzwilliam on the phone and tell him we want to see his mother's death certificate," and before he had time to think the Sergeant replied:

"I've got Mr Fitzwilliam on the line. Did you want to speak to him?"

Harry was the type of man who could never wait in a queue. If he went to the bank or post office and queues had formed, he would march up to the foreign currency counter, or any counter that did not have a queue. After some spurious enquiry he would divulge the real reason for his being there with a "Drop this in for me Jenny," or "Give us a couple of stamps, there's a good girl." It worked for the superintendent because he was well known and the chief policeman in the area. And so it was with his questioning: straight, that was Harry's way.

"Hello Mr Fitzwilliam, I want to see your mother's death certificate, please. Can you bring it in smartish? Of course she was aware her husband was dead when she left the country." It was more a statement than a question.

"Superintendent? Is that Superintendent Furlong?"

"Yes, yes please bring in your mother's death certificate."

"Well of course I will if you need it. Did you read the letter from Maurice Agan? That's what I want to know."

"Mr Fitzwilliam, I will not discuss anything over the phone. Will you be in tomorrow?"

A long silence intervened but the line had not gone dead and Harry decided not to break the silence.

Eventually Paddy said, "Tomorrow then." There was no trepidation in his voice, just irritation.

"Sergeant," Harry bellowed down the stairs. "Come up for a moment!" No memory disturbed his conscience of having so often and so vehemently told all and sundry that there should be no roaring up or down the stairs, no high-pitched calls, no whistles for attention, but only the civilised and restrained use of the telephone.

He waited impatiently for the Sergeant's heavy footsteps on the wooden staircase. The Sergeant needed a kicking, but he had an excellent recall of all the great and not so great happenings, and that was all that Furlong was interested in just now.

"Now then Sergeant; know anything of that new Mrs up at Tuskar?"

"Nothing comes to mind, you know. Keeps herself to herself. Did hear she had a bit of an affair with Tom Fitzwilliam. That was before she married into the Agan family."

"What a nuisance that man was around the area, upsetting all. I've heard he was well named: Tomcat."

"Hah! He was that all right."

"Did ye hear any word about a letter that Maurice Agan might have written to his daughter? The daughter talked to me about it but then seemed to change her mind about showing it to me, and now Paddy Fitzwilliam appears to have got interested in it?"

The sergeant shook his head. He was longing to know more but the Superintendent went on quickly. "Well! You remember when Liadan Agan said she had seen a dead person at the lake, must be 8 years ago? She was a child then and nobody paid much attention to her, but when ye look back at the thing, just, indeed, because she was a child, she was probably telling the truth and now she is covering something up. Mrs Agan said she had burnt the letter from her husband, or she hinted as much," Harry continued. He was now in fact talking to himself but the sergeant continued to stand in the doorway.

The superintendent shook his head: "That troubled, tousled-haired girl looked desperately close to tears. I expect it means she believed her stepmother had actually burnt the letter and maybe not at her bidding either. Could it be that the stepmother wanted to confuse the issue?" Harry thought, forgetting all about the sergeant.

Suddenly the sergeant interrupted this train of thought. "I didn't know Mrs Agan personally, but gossip has it that she and Tom met often at the Fitzwilliam's and that Maurice Agan was always jealous, forever ranting and raving about the town..."

"That'll be all Sergeant." The superintendent abruptly became aware of the sergeant's presence and just as immediately tired of it.

"Maurice Agan? He'd had a lot in common with Maurice, or did he? Not the wealth of course, nor the standing, but few people were better company than Maurice over a pint in Seals. Tom, on the other hand, not the same fish... charismatic though... interested in everybody."

"Maybe there's no letter at all, just a figment of the girl's imagination. But then why would the stepmother answer so "pat" that she had burned it?" Harry thought. He allowed his empty mug to slip from his fingers on to his desk. He was tired but afraid to let go of his thoughts. "What have we got? Tom was quite a man with the ladies; known to all and sundry including the sergeant."

"I wonder," he asked himself, "why Liadan was so worried about Paddy? What's going on between them? Perhaps it was Paddy she was trying to protect. Perhaps…"

"Yes, I think I see." The Inspector began to think out loud again. "Where is that rifle? Find the rifle and we'll have our man. If it's not in the lake and it's not in the shelter…we'll never find it…. the rifle might have gone to Kenya. Oh dear, oh dear!"

"Sergeant!" and this time Harry did pick up the phone. "Get someone over to the Fitzwilliam's place, to Pastures New, and have the house searched completely - outhouses included, even attics."

Harry snarled a bit to himself; he had a cold and sore head. He thought he might go home for a while. High above street-level his little window looked out on a leaden sky. He had hoped for snow, tons of it: any excuse to get home to bed, a hot toddy and not wake up until Friday. Last year it had snowed for the first time in March, so anything was possible. The finished reports would not be in for a couple of days. His head throbbed, his sinuses ached, his ears were red hot. What else could he do? A follow-up interview with Liadan and her stepmother maybe… one of the female Garda should be there, just in case things got emotional.

A flurry softly drifted past the window and for a moment Harry felt he had actually ordered the snow, but before he had time to express his gratitude, the snow had stopped falling.

Could there be any connection between the two deaths – Tom Fitzwilliam's and the young girl, Anna's? It all seemed a bit far-fetched. Anna had died because of her *anorexia nervosa*, and this had recently taken a couple of young lives in the town, but it was hardly anything to do with Tom Fitzwilliam… surely not? He sighed deeply and his headache throbbed insistently. He felt that he should examine both of the families involved more closely, but he was at a loss to know where to begin. He vaguely surmised that a more psychological approach might reveal things that were at present being missed: he had noticed that when Paddy talked of the Agans his voice became strained, muffled and lower-pitched, as if he were talking to himself and not wishing to be heard; as though he were touching on some deep and tormenting idea. "After all", he thought, the headache lifting a little with the feeling of satisfaction, "reading people was his *forte*." Harry Furlong slowly but deftly rose from his desk, gained possession of his hat and coat and faced calmly out into another flurry of soft and gently falling flakes, moving contentedly towards home and warmth.

Chapter 19

1984

"Anything?" the superintendent asked, and then again impatiently "Well, what have you got?"

"Nothing...absolutely nothing!" the sergeant replied in a sulky voice. Standing behind his desk he rummaged in a cabinet drawer, as if expecting to find something there.

"What about the girl, Liadan Agan, then? Did she come in with that letter?"

"Nope ...no letter... I'd love to know what really happened... It's a close day today, isn't it?"

"And the search at Pastures New?" the superintendent continued to query, ignoring the sergeant's remark. He did indeed often wonder how he put up with the sergeant, who seemed frequently to show a very frivolous side when dealing with matters of obvious seriousness. What had the closeness of the day to do with the business in hand? He then remembered the time that the old Widow Connery had disappeared and the alarm was raised immediately by her daughter. The sergeant, to the intense irritation of the superintendent, kept insisting on the deliciousness of the Widow Connery's cakes and sure enough the Widow was found wandering dementedly around a town that she used to go to years before to buy some mysterious ingredient which gave her cakes the very deliciousness the sergeant had so robustly put forward.

"Paddy Fitzwilliam said he didn't see a rifle, although he admits his mother owned one. She liked wood-pigeon shooting. But he said there was no shooting at the lakeside that day. You know, there is a rifle still licensed out in Mrs Fitzwilliam's name. I gather it was done automatically by the firm that looked after the place while the Fitzwilliams were away."

"Get Paddy in," Harry said. He ran up the stairs.

He threw a file on to his desk. " John Cullen down by the Fort has a very interesting case. He'd appreciate a bit of extra help and I told him we would be winding this one up shortly." He mused to himself. "Fat chance of that. If I find out the cause of the row at the lake, surely that'll crack this case." He tried to encourage himself and yet underneath it all he felt that there was an intangible aspect to the whole story and that whatever it was – the key to the whole thing lay where nobody had yet looked.

A sleepy atmosphere had descended on the town and the noise of the traffic was subdued to a mere hum coming from the street above him. He had noticed a gossipy sort of whispering everywhere he went and he had started to suspect that some of them thought he was being a bit slow: some thought the obvious was beyond him; they were quite humorous. "We all knew it was Tom Fitzwilliam, so we did." Oh yes they had known the remains would be of Tom Fitzwilliam, even before the superintendent had known: "'Cos it stood to reason, who else had disappeared?" Elsie Draper had vanished a few years ago, but she had been found in England, safe and sound with a fast-growing family. There were another couple of temporarily mysterious disappearances, but they had all been accounted for.

George Collins, Delia's husband, had slapped him on the back; "We'll do all the work for you, never fear," he had promised.

Another mad hatter had foretold the imminent appearance of another body.

"And Lo! Tom Fitzwilliam rose up again and smote his enemies." Harry thought. How they would like that.

Cross and irritated he picked up the phone: "Get the whole lot of them in here asap: Felicity and Liadan Agan, Paddy Fitzwilliam and... that Wendy Leigh – she was a friend of both families. Get one of the Guards to chat up some of the locals: I would suggest Delia Collins as a good start and that one in the Café. OK, get on with it," Harry got in quickly before the sergeant had time to answer back.

* * *

"Did you hear love? I've found a home for the kitties …the last lot of the poor little things. They're coming for them this afternoon."

But Liadan wasn't interested and she left the kitchen.

***

When she returned later that afternoon she found the kitchen in chaos with Lucy, still in her coat, just back from the police station, or so she was just announcing to Felicity, who sat at the table drinking tea from a mug in a bemused state, while Lucy walked up and down remarking under her breath, in a conciliatory way, "It's a fact." Liadan was fascinated by the scene: it seemed to her that, after so many years of struggle, they had finally bonded. They both helped Liadan to tea.

"That couple came for the kittens and I showed them where they were meself – up in the cowshed. I'd asked Charley to show them, but he's useless at that sort of thing. He had that look on his face which told me that he might and then he mightn't."

Felicity smiled encouragingly and Liadan said "So …?"

"Let me draw me breath…" She took a sip of tea. "Anyway… the kitties were in the stall opposite the door as snug as bugs … Mother was no trouble and purred all the time."

Felicity continued to smile but Liadan couldn't contain herself.

"*Lucyee please…*"

"Patience was never one o' your virtues," Lucy said crossly. "Anyway, I thought there should be another kitty and then your man puts his hand down into the manger and found the third. We were delighted. But the kitty was all tied up in a scarf; up came the scarf and then I noticed something stickin' out o' the hay…a rifle…God bless me…God help me!" Lucy's voice got shrill and her mouth stretched tightly over her teeth.

No one spoke. Liadan's eyes had taken over her face.

"I gave it a good clean before I gave it to the police."

"Yes, she did." Felicity said in exact mimicry of Lucy's stricken voice.

"Maybe you shouldn't have done that." Liadan said, hardly knowing she spoke.

"The couple gave me a lift to the station…" Lucy went on ignoring her.

"You took the rifle to the police then?" Liadan managed.

"There was no hidin' it." Lucy eyes looked steely.

***

"Let's take things calmly, as far as we can." Superintendent Furlong spoke aloud to stem his own edginess. "Why didn't Paddy tell all this sooner," he grumbled under his breath. "That Wendy girl, I expect," he answered himself.

The superintendent and the sergeant stood on the steps up to the front door of Tuskar House. Lucy's find had changed everything. Paddy had come running to the Garda station with Wendy. He was willing now to tell all that he knew.

"Ok, I did get a letter: a written confession from my father." Liadan had thrown open the door and poked the superintendent in the chest. Now she too was jumping to tell, Harry thought.

"I'll show it to you. He had nothing to do with the rifle… nothing. "

"I know."

He believed her. Wendy and Paddy had told him. They moved into the house, following Liadan down the bare hallway, each footstep a remembered sound. But he noticed straight away how she walked steadily and easily even though she must have been worried. A change had taken place in the young girl. Doors were still wide open into large rooms along the hallway. The windows of the rooms were themselves thrown open to the April evening air, but, as before, they were empty of anything except majestic space and fading sunshine. Near the end of the hall Liadan paused and said to him:

" Please wait in here… I'll fetch the letter", and she opened the door to a room.

Superintendent Furlong and the sergeant expected to enter another empty room but found it to be furnished and occupied.

"This is my solicitor, Ronan Dalkey." Liadan explained and then, as an afterthought, "He's also my fiancé. " She smiled at Ronan so lovingly it warmed the superintendent's heart.

Harry Furlong took Ronan's hand cordially. They would be able to tell her everything about the conclusions that they had come to. Good old Ronan would be there to support her. Of course, Paddy had changed his tale a couple of times; he was a badly hurt man. They had got the truth finally, Harry felt sure. Wendy confirmed everything. Anna had told her everything.

"Good," he said.

As the superintendent read the letter his grave face became graver. It shook him that Maurice Agan had written such a letter to his daughter, but then he thought that he understood the logic behind it. On a second reading he noted how the rifle had been thrown on the ground almost forgotten - so curious. No mention of a shooting; it was all adding up. And Anna! He felt sure that the matter of Anna explained why it had ended as it had.

"Would it be possible to speak to your mother?" he asked Liadan. "Just to confirm one or two points."

Liadan looked at him pointedly, waiting for something.

"Eh, your step-mother." The sergeant was delighted to be able to correct his superior.

"You can speak to her now," the girl answered, "She's out in the garden."

They walked out on to the veranda, the four of them, with a fifth shadowy figure, Lucy, lingering in the background.

The superintendent surveyed the beautiful garden while he waited for the little group to assemble. He looked towards the old beech trees, standing like great honourable dignitaries, their vast branches throwing a gentle and restoring shade over the lawn; their grave bearing inspiring confidence; their quiet movement and fine branches relieving and assuaging. "How" he wondered, "could such things come about in a place like this?" He wished it were all over now. In every job of this kind this was the point to be most dreaded. But here it must surely be worse: to tell the unsuspected things they would never have thought they would have to hear.

When they had all gathered they returned to the drawing-room and he began immediately. He went though the whole sorry tale as concisely and clearly as possible, almost as if he had learnt it by heart and when he had finished he waited to try to give the poor girl some extra time to compose herself. He was ready to explain anything if he were asked.

" Paddy and Wendy both agreed that you might not know about Anna. It seems very probable that Mrs Fitzwilliam knew. She may have followed her husband to the lake that day. It was her scarf that was twisted around the rifle which was licensed and belonged to her. On the scarf there was some very identifiable purple nail varnish staining the fabric. Paddy seemed reluctant but agreed it might be his mother's." The superintendent waited again before finishing off: "We are not going any further with this. There isn't any point."

Liadan's transfixed look convinced him she had not known much. He had never seen, except in the case of actual physical violence, a girl more shaken than this one. Her eyes were almost blank with horror and then after a few seconds the horror turned to a look of questioning fear and then, as though she had again become aware of those around her, her expression changed to a despairing acceptance: there was no choice now but to accept, for how could such things be worked out, be talked of, be even mentioned when those ... She looked around, her lips trembling and she smiled:

"I think I had begun to suspect," she said. "I'm all right. I'm really all right."

Everything had been said; it was time now for the superintendent and sergeant to leave. All the others were quiet. Lucy asked for a lift to the bottom of the long avenue and Felicity had risen to go to her bedroom. "Now we all *know*," she had said to them before making her way up the stairs towards the dying light that streamed in through the landing windows.

CHAPTER 20

When Anna danced people watched. The celandine carpet was gone from the drawing-room and the veranda doors were flung open. Faster and faster she danced, dragging Paddy on to the floor. Anna danced with John, tall, slightly stooped, smiling John. Liadan watched with wonder her sister's gyrating feet. They were laughing and clapping. Liadan tapped the wood on the piano wishing she could dance, wishing she were older. Anna grabbed her hand. Carefree, her feet hardly touching the floor, she danced, drawing Liadan around the room and throwing her gently into the arms of John. When Anna stopped dancing her friends crowded round her, talking in animated voices. Her eyes touched on each; no one was excluded. Liadan watched in admiration at how she made them all her special friends. Anna looked giddy with joy.

Out on the dark-ringed lawn the young ones held hands or ran around unable to contain their juvenescent, exuberant spirits. Laughter rang out over the lawn even down to the river where Liadan went to look for her lost racquet. The smell of honeysuckle wafted its way over their heads and seemed to gain force afresh from the moist lawn. Bands of light lit the grass and pathways of music filled the air. Summer light had faded beautifully away and a moon shone down on hearts bursting with the wonder of it all; unpaired young ones sat close together waiting in hope, their youthful hearts pounding.

Liadan came back without her racquet to sit with Paddy; the little girl laid her head upon his shoulder. He ran his fingers through her hair in an absent-minded way as he talked to his friends. She had fallen asleep in his arms when Maurice eventually came to take her to bed.

"If you're staying the night, camp on the floor in the sitting-room," he announced to everyone. "We're going to bed."

Maurice hoped Paddy would go home. He was tired of his mother ringing up and that man Tom's insufferable insinuations of what Paddy and Anna might get up to. For a moment he wondered where Anna might be. Busy organising, he suspected.

"We'll be working tomorrow. Come along Angel" he spoke softly to his daughter. "You need to get to bed; even Felicity's gone there," he said to encourage her.

"No, she's not Daddy." Liadan said very definitely, but he smiled.

Bit by bit the house closed down and the quiet of the countryside slipped onto the emptying lawn.

* * *

Tom watched as Anna stole from the house – he knew it was her when the shadows moved.

He was so close he could hear her breathing. She crept under the laurel bushes, tripping in her haste over the twisted branches. He had watched her so many times before on the secret hidden route to the lake. She sniffed the air like a young deer. Sometimes when he had watched she had seemed to know he was there, although they never spoke. It had been plain to Tom that she would go to the lake that night and that they would meet. They had communicated over the heads of everyone with talk of midnight meetings and poetry.

Quietly he stalked her, moving with more steadiness than her dashing feet. He saw her pause at the kissing gate. She must have heard the lapping of the lake waters on the stones. At night sounds like these were clearer in the summer months and seemed to linger in the air, somehow a part of the urging of nature within them. Throwing back her head she ran down to the lake reaching the water before him.

She threw her clothes upon the ground and jumped into the cold water before he could catch hold of her. When they emerged from the water they were entwined in a long lover's kiss.